𝔪𝔟𝔰

ACCLAIM FOR COLLEEN COBLE

"I burned through *The Inn at Ocean's Edge* in one sitting. An intricate plot by a master storyteller. Colleen Coble has done it again with this gripping opening to a new series. I can't wait to spend more time at Sunset Cove."

—Heather Burch, bestselling author of *One Lavender Ribbon*

"Coble doesn't disappoint with her custom blend of suspense and romance."

—*Publishers Weekly* for *The Inn at Ocean's Edge*

"Veteran author Coble has penned another winner. Filled with mystery and romance that are unpredictable until the last page, this novel will grip readers long past when they should put their books down. Recommended to readers of contemporary mysteries."

—*CBA Retailers + Resources*

"Coble truly shines when she's penning a mystery, and this tale will really keep the reader guessing . . . Mystery lovers will definitely want to put this book on their purchase list."

—*Romantic Times* Book Reviews

"Master storyteller Colleen Coble has done it again. *The Inn at Ocean's Edge* is an intricately woven, well-crafted story of romance, suspense, family secrets, and a decades old mystery. Needless to say, it had me hooked from page one. I simply couldn't stop turning the pages. This one's going on my keeper shelf."

—Lynette Eason, award-winning,
bestselling author of the Hidden Identity series

"Evocative and gripping, *The Inn at Ocean's Edge* will keep you flipping pages long into the night."

—Dani Pettrey, bestselling author of
the Alaskan Courage series

"Coble's atmospheric and suspenseful series launch should appeal to fans of Tracie Peterson and other authors of Christian romantic suspense."

—*Library Journal* review of *Tidewater Inn*

ALL IS CALM,
ALL IS BRIGHT

ALSO BY COLLEEN COBLE

ALL IS CALM,
ALL IS BRIGHT

A Colleen Coble Christmas Collection

COLLEEN COBLE

THOMAS NELSON
Since 1798

Published in Nashville, Tennessee, by Thomas Nelson. Thomas Nelson is a registered trademark of HarperCollins Christian Publishing, Inc.

Thomas Nelson titles may be purchased in bulk for educational, business, fund-raising, or sales promotional use. For information, please e-mail SpecialMarkets@ThomasNelson.com.

Library of Congress Cataloging-in-Publication Data is available upon request.

ISBN: 978-0-7180-3782-6

15 16 17 18 19 20 / RRD / 21 20 19 18 17 16 15 14 13 12 11 10 9 8 7 6 5 4 3 2 1

Contents

ALL IS CALM

ONE

THIS IS WRONG ON EVERY COUNT. CHRISTMAS WAS THREE WEEKS away. Did that mean nothing to these men? Lauren Everman darted into the barn and locked the padlock from the inside. Angel, the black stallion behind her, snorted when she rattled the chain to make sure it held.

"Lauren, you unlock this door right now." Ranch owner Charles McLeod yelled from outside the barn. "You know it has to be done."

"It wasn't his fault!" She backed away from the door and went to stand near Angel's stall. "It's okay, boy. I won't let anyone hurt you."

"The vet can't stay any longer. We can do this nice and humane, or I'll just have to shoot him later." Her boss pounded on the door.

"I'm telling you it wasn't his fault. Someone shot him full of some kind of drug. I saw it." She had no real hope McLeod would listen to her. Trouble always seemed to find her no matter what she did or how hard she tried. She'd already tried to tell him about the shadowy figures she'd seen two days ago and the bullet that had come whizzing by her head. He claimed she was being dramatic and just wanted attention. She knew better. "Angel would never hurt anyone on purpose."

As if to contradict her, the stallion bit down on her arm hard enough to make her wince. She jerked out of his way. Poor fellow. Angel was stressed. She moved down the length of the stall and checked the back door to make sure it was securely locked. It was. So were the windows. No one was getting in here unless she let them.

McLeod shouted her name again, then peered through the window at her. She turned her back on him and flopped down in the hay. Might as well make herself comfortable. It was going to be a long night.

Through one window the sunset put on a spectacular show. She focused on it and tried to tune out the angry men outside. They couldn't kill Angel . . . They just couldn't. She'd never be able to live with the injustice of it.

An idea began to foment. What if she escaped with him and went far away where they'd never find him? With Tonia's lies, the police had been questioning her about Dustin's death as if she was a suspect. But where could she go to find a safe haven?

Bluebird Ranch. The notion popped into her head. She'd spent a life-changing summer there twelve years ago when she was seventeen. It was a terrific ranch that paired abused children with abused horses. When she was a foster kid, the place had been the one bright spot for her. There was always a place there for a good horse and a hard worker. She could get there in a day. All she had to do was get to El Paso, then head east to the Big Bend area of West Texas.

She got up and dusted the hay off her jeans. She couldn't just steal the horse, though. The horse was worth ten grand. On second thought, if McLeod was prepared to put him down anyway, any money he got should make him happy.

Her heart singing, she practically ran to her room, a tiny space in the back of the barn, and dug out her checkbook. She wrote out a check for five thousand dollars, nearly cleaning out her account, and tucked the corner of the check under a lamp on the nightstand.

Once they left her in peace, she'd make her getaway under cover of night. She grabbed her Stetson. It wouldn't be the first time she'd run.

～♒～

Brendan Waddell had always considered the Bluebird Ranch a little piece of heaven, and today was no exception when he parked his truck in the dirt drive and got out. He drew in a deep breath of mesquite and creosote, the finest scent on earth as far as he was concerned. The twinkling Christmas lights welcomed him.

Allie Bailey, Rick's petite wife, bounced down the porch steps before he even managed to shut the door behind him. "You're late."

Her tight hug told him he was welcome. "Had to stop for

gas." And to walk off the pain gripping his right leg, but he wasn't about to tell her that. He released her and stepped back, eyeing the huge tummy bulge under her sleeveless red top. "You look like you're about to pop."

Her bright blue eyes widened. "How ungentlemanly of you to notice." Her laugh rang out. "It's a girl this time, due end of December."

"I bet Rick is over the moon."

"Sure is. We both want a big family." He followed her toward the house, a sprawling home typical of its West Texas setting. White barns, outbuildings, and bunkhouses ranged over the property. This place was exactly what he needed.

A young woman pushing a child in a tire swing under a large mesquite tree caught his attention. He'd seen her before somewhere, hadn't he? Or a picture of her maybe? In his intelligence position with Special Ops, he read every bit of local news and unusual circumstances that came across his desk. She didn't seem to notice him staring as she pushed the little girl higher and higher.

He nodded toward the two. "Who's that?"

"Interested? I think she's single." Allie's impudent grin flashed up at him.

Used to friends trying to marry him off, Brendan kept his face impassive. If he ignored the innuendos, they'd leave him alone sooner or later. "She just looks familiar. Was she here last time I came?"

Allie shook her head as she mounted the steps to the house. "Lauren just arrived a couple of days ago looking for a job. She was a guest here years ago when she was a teenager. As luck would have it, we were in need of a new horse trainer. She's amazing with horses. It's like she speaks their language. Her letters of recommendation were impeccable, and Rick hired her on the spot."

He spared one last glance at the brunette. The ponytail holding her dark hair emphasized her high cheekbones and expressive dark brown eyes. She looked over and caught his gaze. A tinge of color sprang to her face, and she turned away to attend to the little girl.

"Her kid?"

"No, one of our foster kids here for the summer." Allie opened the screen door. "Rick will be home in a few minutes. He ran to the feed store."

When Brendan entered the living room, a whirlwind attacked his good leg. He lifted the four-year-old into his arms, and little Matthew clung like a monkey. "Hey, squirt."

The little boy puffed out his chest. "I'm not a squirt anymore, Uncle Brendan. I'm big."

"You've grown two inches since I saw you." Brendan set him back on the floor and lifted a brow in Allie's direction. "My usual room?"

"It's all ready for you."

"I'll be right back." He sniffed the air, redolent with the aroma of Mexican spices. "Smells like enchiladas." His stomach rumbled.

Allie smiled and took her son's hand. "You nailed it."

Brendan went down the hall and dropped his luggage, then headed for the kitchen.

Allie nodded out the window. "Rick just got back. Have a seat, and we'll eat."

"I'm starved." He pulled out a chair beside Matthew.

The front door banged, and he rose to greet Rick. The two had been in the Marines together before Rick got out and came home to West Texas. Brendan had gone on to bigger and better things with the intelligence division, or so he'd thought at the time. Now, looking at the happy family around him, Brendan wasn't so sure what he should decide this time. He could take a medical discharge or fight it and end up pushing papers the rest of his military career.

Rick hadn't changed much in the ten years they'd been friends. There were a few more lines around his blue eyes, but his rangy form was just as lean and muscular as ever.

As Brendan shook Rick's hand, he noticed another figure behind him. Lauren, the woman from the front yard. Their gazes locked for a moment, then she ducked her head and went to pull out the chair at the other end of the table.

Rick glanced her way. "Lauren, he's not as surly as he seems. Smile, Brendan. I know you know how."

Brendan blinked, then managed a grin. "I promise not to bite."

Lauren's gaze came up, and a tiny smile lifted her lips. She was really a knockout up close. Perfect olive skin and eyes fringed with thick lashes.

"Where you from, Lauren?" He put the question out with practiced charm.

She bit her lip and looked down at her plate. "Dallas area."

What was she hiding? He could sniff out deception a mile away. "You don't have much of a Texas accent."

"Originally from Indiana. I've just been in Dallas three years."

"You're a horse trainer?"

Her nod came, barely discernible. "I love horses."

Rick pulled out a chair beside his son. "She brought a stallion with her. We've already had a neighbor ask to use him as a stud. He's gorgeous."

A genuine smile brightened Lauren's face. "I fell in love with him the first time I saw him. Everyone was afraid of him, but he's a sweetheart."

Allie unfolded her napkin. "I don't know about that. He won't let me within five feet of him. You've got a special touch, Lauren. No horse seems able to resist you. You've got our horses eating out of your palm already. And the children as well. You're like a Pied Piper. I thought we'd have to get rid of Jilly, but she's as docile as can be now."

"I'm glad to be here. It's a wonderful haven."

Brendan considered Bluebird Ranch his haven, too, a place where he could be himself with an old and trusted friend, but what was she running from? There was a darkness in her eyes, some kind of suffering that made him curious. He'd ask Rick about her tonight.

Two

THE GUY PUT HER NERVES ON END. AS SOON AS THE BAILEY family moved to the living room and turned on a Christmas special for little Matthew, Lauren said her good nights and escaped to the sky sprinkled with stars. It was like looking at her own personal Christmas lights. The gravel crunched under her feet as she hurried to her room in the barn. The Baileys had offered her a room in the bunkhouse, but it was full of all guys, and she felt much more comfortable here amid the sweet scent of hay and the pungent odor of horse.

She paused to rub Angel's soft nose, then went to her room and shut the door behind her. The ten-by-twelve space held a cot, an upside-down crate that served as a bedside table, and a battered white dresser. A door opened into a tiny bathroom with a rust-stained shower barely big enough to turn around in. She'd loved it immediately.

She pulled on pajamas, washed off her makeup, then braided her hair before grabbing her e-reader and crawling into bed. She'd barely flipped it on when a noise caused her to bolt upright. *Someone is out there.*

She scrambled out of bed and stepped to the door. Was that breathing on the other side? Her heart thumped hard in her chest. Someone was there, she just knew it. She glanced around for a weapon. Once upon a time, she'd had a gun—until she pawned it. Now all she had were her cuticle scissors, but she was strong. If she jabbed the point into someone, it might be enough to allow her to get away.

She grabbed the small scissors from the top of her bedside table, then stepped back to the door. She held up the scissors and flung open the door. Brendan took a step back.

His eyes widened when they took in the cuticle scissors in her upraised hand. His lips twitched. "If I wanted to hurt you, you'd be on the floor in five seconds flat. Those little things wouldn't help you at all."

"I could put your eye out."

He shoved his hands in his pockets and leaned against the doorjamb. "I didn't mean to scare you."

"You could have called out. What do you want?"

"I asked Rick about you. Last name is Everman, not a common name. I knew you looked familiar. Law enforcement has been looking for you for two months in connection with the death of that jockey Dustin Windsor."

How did he know this? It wasn't like the search was on national news stations. Her throat too tight to speak, she brushed past him and went to check on Angel. Brendan followed her, crowding into her personal space so far that she whirled and shoved his chest. "Back off!"

His brows rose. "You can't blame me for wanting to protect my friends. This a stolen racehorse?"

"I paid for him!" But her cheeks heated when she realized she'd admitted he was a racehorse. "He's past his prime now. They were going to put him down. They blamed him for Dustin's death, but it wasn't his fault." She hated herself for the whine in her tone and straightened her shoulders. "I was happy to buy him and bring him to a new life. *My* new life."

"As long as there aren't still remnants of your old life that might threaten my friends." His mild voice held a steely undertone. "Why are you here?"

"Did you say anything to Rick and Allie?"

"Not yet. I wanted to hear from you."

"I wasn't guilty of anything. I just wanted to get Angel away from there."

"Innocent, huh? That's what everyone says."

His cynicism made her throat close. People always believed the worst. She believed everyone deserved to be heard, but this cold-eyed man wasn't going to listen to a thing she said. He'd judged her and found her guilty.

She swallowed hard. "You can't tell anyone I'm here. If you do, my death will be on your head."

He straightened. "Your death?"

She nodded and blinked back the moisture in her eyes. "They think I can identify Dustin's killer. I started getting threatening calls."

"Tell me what happened."

She turned and rubbed Angel's soft nose. The scent of horse soothed her and drained the tension from her shoulders. How on earth did she tell this stranger her fears?

"The best thing is to turn yourself in and tell what you know."

"Best for whom? My own cousin—" Angel must have felt her returning tension because he jerked his head away and snorted. She held out her hand. "Easy, boy."

"What about your cousin?"

"Nothing." This intense man wouldn't understand her sense of betrayal. He clearly dealt only with the facts. Her eyes burned again and she looked away.

His hand touched her shoulder, and she turned to look at him. Did she dare believe the bit of sympathy in his brown eyes? Or was it merely a ploy to get her to open up?

"I know a little about betrayal. Who is this cousin and what did he do?"

Betrayal. That's why this hurt so much. She saw the truth of his own pain in his eyes. Maybe she could trust him to get it. She so badly needed to confide in someone. It was hard to force this pain down.

"She." She cleared her throat. "Tonia was with the man who broke into the barn the night Dustin was killed. I saw her, but I didn't tell the police."

"Why not?"

She shrugged. "I didn't want anything bad to happen to her."

"But she claimed *you* let that man in. To throw suspicion off herself?"

"I guess." She looked down at her hands. "I would never rat her out. Even now, you're the first person I've told."

"Tell me exactly what you saw the night of the murder." He was all business now with his expression somber and intent.

She closed her eyes, remembering that night, then opened them and stared into his handsome face. "I was the stable manager and trainer for Charles McLeod. I was working late that night because of a foaling mare. I had the lights off to soothe her, and I was tired since I'd been up the night before too. I must have dozed off. A noise awakened me, and I got up and went to the window. I saw Tonia with a guy in a big black truck. When I turned back around, I saw a hooded figure moving quickly through the barn. Then I saw Dustin lying on the hay. The hay was wet with blood."

"I thought you said there were no lights."

"The moon was shining through the windows." She wet her lips. "The man strode past me, and I saw a hypodermic needle in his hand. He was heading toward McLeod's prize horse, Elijah. Angel was already going crazy and striking Dustin with his hooves. I think the man had already given him a shot of something."

"This man, he didn't see you?"

"Not at first. I looked around for a weapon and grabbed a shovel. When he got close enough, I hit him with it. When he fell to the ground, I ran to the door and shouted for help." She well remembered the terror of that night, the way her scream echoed into the cold night air, the way the lights flashed on in the bunkhouse and men came running. The shrieking of the fire trucks out on a fire run somewhere. "I took McLeod back to the barn where I'd knocked out the intruder, but he was gone."

"I assume the police came that night?"

She nodded. "I told them what I'd seen and who all was there. But the next day when they asked what she'd seen, Tonia told them she'd seen me with some guy, that I'd let him in the barn. That I was involved."

"Why would she do that? What motive would she have for lying?"

A wealth of reasons. How did she even start to tell him about Tonia's building jealousy? "It's complicated. I doubt you could understand. I don't even get it."

"Try me."

"Her one goal in life was to marry well. She wanted a man with money and prestige, and she seemed to have found him in Steve McAvoy."

"The state senator?"

"That's the one. She thought he was going to propose." She looked down at her hands. "Then she brought him to the track and we met. After that he wouldn't leave me alone. I told him I wasn't interested, but he wouldn't listen." The words rushed out, faster and faster. "He started sending me flowers, candy, jewelry. I refused all of it, but then he started waiting for me by my car every night."

"Tonia found out?"

Lauren gave a jerky nod. "She was furious with me. He finally seemed to understand I wasn't interested and went back to Tonia. She's still not speaking to me, but at least she's happy."

"And you never told the police you saw her that night?"

She shook her head. "It would just be my word against hers. Besides, I couldn't do that to her. She didn't have anything to do with Dustin's death."

He lifted a brow. "Back to the murder. What would have been in that needle?"

"Cocaine. The investigation revealed a drug in Angel's blood."

"And what about Angel? He was blamed for the death, at least until the autopsy came back, right? And then it showed Windsor had been killed by a massive overdose of cocaine."

He'd done his homework. She nodded.

"So you think Tonia took this chance to implicate you in a crime so she could make sure you didn't tempt McAvoy ever again?"

Lauren pressed her lips together at the skepticism in his voice. Put so baldly it did seem outrageous. "I think so, yes. Why else would she lie like that?"

He didn't have to answer. She knew he was thinking that Tonia didn't lie—that Lauren had really been involved in Windsor's death. She saw it in the way he stepped back a bit and shuttered his eyes.

"Please, you have to believe me. I had nothing to do with Dustin's death. I don't know who did it, and I didn't let anyone into the barn." He'd never believe her. She might as well pack her bags now and try to find another safe place to land before he called in the authorities.

She turned on her heels and headed toward the barn.

A coyote yipped in the darkness outside the living room window. Brendan rubbed his burning eyes and stared at the laptop screen. "There isn't much on the murder. The investigation seems to have gone nowhere."

Rick sat on the sofa with his arm around Allie, who had fallen asleep with her head on his shoulder. "I don't think she's guilty of anything."

"So you've already said. The sketchy details point to her guilt."

"I called all her references, and they raved about her. And horses seem to have a sixth sense about character."

Brendan barely refrained from rolling his eyes. He wanted more to go on than some animal's sixth sense. "According to her bio here, she grew up in Nashville. Her mom was raising her cousin Tonia too, and both girls ended up in foster care when her mom died of cancer. Lauren was fifteen and Tonia was fourteen."

"Why are you so interested, Brendan? We trust her and want to help her. That's what we do here at the Bluebird. Let's talk about you for a minute."

He stiffened. "There's nothing to talk about. I got shot on a mission, but my leg is doing fine. End of discussion."

"You're still limping." His buddy's blue eyes missed nothing. "It's been what—two months?"

"The doctors say it can take a while to fully heal. I just have to keep doing my physical therapy."

Rick raised a brow. "You're worried you may never be the same, aren't you? That you'll have to give up your career and will end up behind a desk. The one thing you swore would never happen."

Brendan's gut tightened, and his fingers curled into his palms. "I'll be fine. No reason to get all teary eyed over a little bullet. I'll be back to work in six months." Even he could hear the desperation in his voice. What would he do if he couldn't get back to his team? Special Ops was his life. He thrived on the challenge, the rescue missions.

"Everyone's life changes eventually. I didn't want to get out of the military when I did either, but it was time. Turned out to be the best thing that ever happened to me. You'll never have a normal life with a wife and kids while you're traipsing all over the globe. And you're thirty-five. Eventually we can't do what we did when we were twenty-one."

He held up his hand when Brendan started to object. "I know, I know. Every man in your family has ended up leaving his wife and kids. But you're not that kind of man. Maybe this was God's way of slowing you down and making you look at your life."

"My life was just fine before this injury, and it will be again." But Brendan couldn't deny that Rick's words described a quiet longing in his heart. He'd been—lonely. The restless feeling had started before he was wounded. It was getting harder and harder to shove away. "I appreciate your concern, buddy, but I'm fine." He forced a light tone into his voice.

Rick's expression softened. "Change is hard. And the more

we kick against it, the harder we make it on ourselves. When things change, I try to see what good might be in what seems to be awful."

"Try walking with a limp for a few months, and see if you can find anything good in that."

"Physical problems are the worst." Rick shifted and adjusted Allie's head. "But pain makes us more dependent on God." He shrugged. "Easy enough for me to say, I know, sitting here with no physical problems. You say you deal in facts, and that's a good thing. But don't discount your feelings, Brendan. They're an important part of who you are." He nodded toward the computer on Brendan's lap. "What's your gut tell you about Lauren? And don't say it doesn't matter."

Brendan looked down at his computer, which still showed her face and bio. Was it just her beauty that drew him or the hint of sadness in her big brown eyes? She had her arm around a horse and was smiling into the camera, but the shadow in her eyes was there just the same. "I'd like to think she's innocent."

Rick grinned and did a "yes" movement with his fist. "I knew a heart lurked under that logical exterior somewhere."

Brendan grinned back. "Contrary to popular opinion, I'm not Mr. Spock. I just don't like to let emotion cloud my judgment."

"Sometimes it's the best proof we have."

Was it? Brendan tried to remember a time when emotion had directed him to the proper decision and couldn't think of a thing. But then, hadn't he spent his life trying to block out emotion? His father had certainly tried to beat it out of him, and his downtrodden mother hadn't stopped the old man.

"So what's next with Lauren? You going to turn her in?"

He pressed his lips together. "I don't know. I've always upheld the law. Maybe she would remember something that would help the investigation."

"Or maybe they'd be all too ready to blame her, and she'd end up in jail instead. Let's investigate a little on our own. You have access to every kind of information we might need."

"True." Brendan rubbed his head, unsure for the first time what was the right thing to do. "Let's give it until Christmas. If we haven't found good evidence to believe she's innocent, I'll call the detective in charge and let him take over."

A frown crouched between Rick's eyes, but he finally nodded. "Fair enough, I guess. But let's give it a try."

"I never do anything else." He closed his laptop and stood. A light still shone in the barn. He hoped his visit hadn't caused Lauren a sleepless night. "I think I'll tell her what we've decided so she can get some rest."

He ignored Rick's smirk as he headed for the door.

THREE

THE NOVEL WASN'T HOLDING HER ATTENTION. LAUREN flipped off her e-reader and swung her feet to the floor. Maybe some hot cocoa would help. Once she filled the electric teapot and plugged it in, she opened her door to go check on Angel. He'd been a little skittish since they'd fled the McLeod ranch, and a final pat might calm him for the night.

She found the stallion lying in his stall though, so she didn't speak to him. Instead she wandered over to the pile of hay in the far corner and sat for a minute to think. Maybe she should saddle up the horse and escape yet tonight. Brendan thought she was guilty. Once he told Rick, she'd be asked to leave anyway.

The knowledge left a hole in her gut. She shouldn't care what he thought, but she did. It was hard to find condemnation at every turn. What if she called Tonia? Maybe marrying Steve had settled her dissatisfaction with life and she would retract her accusation. It might be worth a try. There was a phone in her room, and Allie had told her even long-distance calls were allowed.

Her heart pulsing in her throat, she went back to her room, added the pouch of chocolate to her mug, and placed the call while she stirred the hot chocolate.

"Hello." Tonia answered, her tone cautious.

Lauren cleared her throat. "Uh, hi, it's me."

"Lauren?" Tonia's voice sharpened. "Where are you?"

Too late Lauren realized her cousin would certainly have caller ID. All she'd have to do was look up the number. "Bluebird, Texas." Maybe her honesty would disarm Tonia.

"What do you want?"

"I saw the wedding announcement last week. I just wanted to congratulate you."

"No thanks to you, was it? I won and you lost."

"It was never a contest, Tonia. You loved him, not me." She bit her lip when her cousin didn't answer. "Listen, I need your help. Can you tell the detective you were wrong about me? That I had nothing to do with the break-in and Dustin's death?"

"Why would I lie for you?"

Lauren gripped the phone hard. "You lied *about* me. You know I didn't meet up with any guy and let him into the barn! I'm sorry I called. You are determined to be vindictive for no good reason. I did nothing to you."

"Nothing? You call trying to steal my boyfriend *nothing*?"

"You'd better keep an eye on your husband, Tonia. He'll need a very short chain if you want to stay married. He has a wandering eye. You're putting the blame in the wrong place."

The click in her ear told her that her cousin had hung up. That had been a waste of her time and effort. She should have known better. Lauren sat on the edge of the bed and buried her face in her hands. The tears she'd kept at bay for so long fell anyway. There was no easy way out of this mess.

When a tap came at her door, she looked up to see Brendan standing in the doorway. "What do you want?" The tears fell faster. He was going to haul her in. She should have left the minute he went back to the house.

"What's wrong?"

"You mean other than the fact everyone believes I did something I didn't do? Or is it that I ran here with nothing but the shirt on my back?" She leaped to her feet and swiped the back of her hand across her wet face. "Forget it. I don't want any pity. I'm fine. And I hate crying." She attempted a watery smile.

He didn't smile back. "I came to tell you Rick knows."

"Oh great." She sank back onto the foot of the bed. "I suppose he wants me to leave."

"No, he wants me to help clear you."

She looked up then and studied the man leaning against the door frame. She had only thought of him as the enemy before now. Brendan was just over six feet tall, and his muscles bulged in his arms and chest, tapering to narrow hips and legs encased in well-worn jeans. A shock of dark hair had the temerity to fall over his forehead, and his brown eyes looked different somehow. Softer, more sympathetic. She guessed him to be in his midthirties. Her gaze dropped to his left hand, which was bare.

She jerked her eyes away. What was she thinking? What difference did his marital status make? "You're going to help me?"

"For now. Rick said to trust my gut, and for some reason I think you're telling me the truth."

She narrowed her eyes. "What do you mean *for now*?"

"I'm going to investigate until Christmas and see if we can figure out what happened to Windsor."

"What happens if you don't find out?"

"We'll call the detective in charge and pull him into the case again."

"And I'll go to jail."

"Maybe not. He might have some new information."

"If he did, you'd already know it, wouldn't you?"

His face changed, and he gave a reluctant nod. "Okay, there's nothing new in the investigation at the moment. But maybe we can jump-start something. Tomorrow let's sit down with Rick and see if you remember something else. Anything that might lead us to what happened that night."

That didn't sound very promising. She'd already told him all she knew, but a slim hope was better than none at all.

⁂

Lauren blinked at the brilliant sunlight when she exited the barn. The scent of sage permeated the air, and the breeze held a crisp edge. She paused when she saw five-year-old Carly Jacobsen. "Hey, sweetheart, did you come to have breakfast with me?" She knelt beside Carly, who stood looking up at her with a somber expression.

Carly nodded and slipped her hand into Lauren's. "Can we have pancakes?"

"It depends on what Cook has prepared. We can walk to the bunkhouse together though." Lauren curled her fingers around the little girl's hand.

She'd felt a deep connection to the child with auburn curls and big green eyes. Allie said no one had been able to make Carly smile. Her file indicated she hadn't laughed since her parents died in a house fire two months earlier. Lauren knew the pain of losing a beloved parent. At least she'd been fifteen and not five.

She didn't have to turn when she heard boots clocking behind her on the stone sidewalk. Only Brendan walked with that military precision he managed in spite of his limp. A tiny frisson of excitement curled in her belly, but she pushed it away. At last someone was going to help her. She could only pray they figured out who had killed Dustin.

He caught up with them. "Where's the fire?"

Carly's fingers convulsed in Lauren's. Lauren narrowed her eyes at him and gave the small fingers a reassuring squeeze. "No fire. We're just going to breakfast." She jerked her head a fraction in Carly's direction and shook her head a bit.

He seemed to catch the unspoken rebuke and glanced at the little girl. "Who's this little cutie?"

Carly kept her head down and didn't speak, so Lauren did. "This is Carly. She's ready for breakfast pancakes. Honey, why don't you run on ahead and save us a table?"

"Okay." Carly pulled her hand from Lauren's and hurried toward the bunkhouse door.

"What's her story? I realized I'd said something wrong when I mentioned a fire."

Lauren told him Carly's tragic story. "So she's afraid of fire, of course. I've made it my personal goal to get her to smile by Christmas."

"Poor kid. Rick and Allie do a lot of good here. How long will she be here?"

"Until the new year, I think. I'm still learning how things work here."

He held open the bunkhouse door for her. "How'd you end up here anyway?"

She contemplated how much she should tell him. "I was here as a foster kid myself once, before Allie and Rick's time. Allie's grandfather ran it back then. It's where I discovered my love of horses, and that experience set me on my career path. I was ready for a change so thought I'd see if they had an opening. They did." Short and sweet.

Brandan's brown eyes missed nothing, and he tipped his head to one side. "I bet there's more to it than that."

She sniffed the air of the cafeteria, noisy with children's chatter. "Smells like maple syrup. Looks like Carly will get her wish for pancakes." She spotted the little girl waving excitedly at a far table. "There she is."

Surely the man could take a hint and would let his questioning drop now. She led the way across the tan tile to the table. Carly was the only child at the table. The other children seemed to ignore her. Friends would help the little girl begin to emerge from the pain of her loss.

She spied another child sitting alone at the next table and beckoned to her. "Summer, come sit with us." The other girl was six, but that was close enough in age for the two to be friends.

Summer's shy smile emerged, and she quickly came to sit beside Carly. "Hi, Carly."

"Hi." Carly's answer was barely audible. She stared at her hands.

Brendan pulled out his chair and sat beside her. "Where are you from, Summer?"

"El Paso. Carly, I'll go with you to get pancakes. We can bring a plate back for Mr. Brendan and Miss Lauren. We can pretend to be servers today."

Carly's head came up and her eyes widened. "Okay." She scooted back her chair and went with Summer to the serving line.

"That was a good idea," Brendan said. "You're good with kids. Have any of your own?"

She shook her head. "I've never been married." Was that a lurking smile? She couldn't deny the pull she had instantly felt toward him. It was surprising and incomprehensible, but maybe he'd felt something too. "How about you?"

"Never had much time for dating or anything. I'm often overseas or flying in or out of hot spots. So no wife and kids for me. Rick and Allie would like to change that." His smile finally did come then. "A happily married couple is constantly pushing others to join their state."

Silence was the best answer now. She smiled to see Carly and Summer heading back their way precariously balancing two plates each. "Looks like we'd better grab our breakfast before it ends up on the floor." She jumped up and took the plate in Summer's left hand.

Brendan reached for his plate from Carly, but before he could rescue it, the stack of pancakes and syrup tilted and landed upside down on his flip-flops. Surprise spread across his face and his eyes went wide.

Carly burst into tears and practically threw her plate onto the table before plopping into her chair. "I'm sorry, Mr. Brendan." She looked down at the ground. "I can't do anything."

He grinned. "You can get a paper towel and help me clean up."

Lauren tore some sheets from the roll on the table and knelt to help clean up the mess.

Carly barely peeked up at him. "You aren't mad?"

"Accidents happen, kiddo. I like syrup so I'll lick it off."

Carly glanced at Lauren, then back to Brendan to see if he was teasing. "I'll clean it." She started to kneel, but he laughed and grabbed her arm.

"I got this, kiddo."

There hadn't been a smile, but Lauren silently thanked Brendan for the lightening of the pain in Carly's eyes.

FOUR

THE CHILDREN WERE ALL IN BED, AND THE FOUR ADULTS SAT IN the living room of the big house. Brendan opened the computer on his lap. "This might be a little uncomfortable, Lauren, but we'll have to poke around into your private life pretty deeply. It may feel intrusive, but I won't be asking questions just to be nosy. Even small details can help me find out more than you think you know about the murder."

Her eyes were apprehensive, and she fidgeted where she sat on the sofa beside Allie. "Okay."

"How long had you worked at the racetrack, and what exactly did you do?"

She relaxed against the back of the sofa. "I was the stable manager for Nelson Stable for six months. It was my job to make sure the horses were fed the proper balance of nutrients and that they were exercised every day."

He typed in her answer in the new document he'd created. "You didn't train them or race them yourself?"

She shook her head. "I had no interest in racing, really. I loved the horses. Beautiful specimens of muscle and spirit."

Brendan glanced at her. "Did something happen to one of them?" He didn't know what made him ask. Maybe it was the way she frowned fiercely down at her hands or how she bit her bottom lip.

She glanced up then, surprise on her face. "Did you read about it?"

Allie glanced at him quickly, and he spotted a smile lifting the corners of her mouth at the concern in his voice. The knowing glint in her eyes caused him to look away. Okay, so Lauren was the prettiest thing he'd seen in, well, maybe ever. Her mixture of spunk and compassion was even more attractive than her glossy dark hair and huge brown eyes. That didn't mean he was going to go down on bended knee.

He lifted a brow in Lauren's general direction. "Nope. So what happened?"

She heaved a sigh. "A horse, Lucky, died in my care." She fell silent a moment. "I'd like to say it wasn't my fault, but I just don't know. I slept right there in the barn, but someone still managed to slip in and give Lucky a shot. He was scheduled to race the next day, and when I went in to check him out before his big day, I couldn't rouse him. He'd foundered, but nothing I fed him could have caused it. The owner fired me on the spot, but before I went to pack my things, I poked around the barn and found a huge sack of grain. Something I'd never purchased for the horses. When we tracked the origin of the sack to a store in Nashville, the owner realized I had nothing to do with it and retracted his dismissal."

"He never found out who had done it?"

She shook her head. "It could have been one of the other horse owners, maybe even the owner of the horse that won the race. A lot of money was riding on that race."

Notating her comment distracted him from how much he liked the melodious sound of her voice. Throaty and compelling. "When was this?"

"About three months . . . before the other thing."

Rick leaned forward. "Dustin Windsor's death. You think the two might be connected?"

"Maybe. Though two different methods were used on the horses. Lucky died after being fed too much grain. Angel was injected with cocaine."

"They were probably hoping people would think your neglect caused Angel's death. I assume he would have died if he hadn't been treated?"

She nodded. "It was a close call as it was. I'm sure they hoped his behavior had caused Dustin's death. And I'm sure it would have come down that way if we'd just found a raging horse in with Dustin."

"What if Windsor hadn't been killed and you'd just woken up to two dead horses? Would you have been able to discover what happened to them? Would a needle prick on the horse be visible to the naked eye?"

"When a horse that valuable dies, there would have been an

autopsy. Foul play is always a possibility, and insurance won't pay out until it has to."

"I'll check into it." Brendan put down the name in his file. "Let's talk about the week leading up to the murder. What did you do that week? Anything unusual stand out in your mind?"

She rubbed her forehead. "Let me think." Her brow furrowed and her eyes sharpened. "I got a couple of hang-ups two nights before the murder. I thought it was just a wrong number at the time."

"What did caller ID show?" Allie asked.

"All that flashed across the screen was Alpine, Texas. No number."

"I assume you didn't report it?" Rick put in.

"No, like I said, I didn't think a thing about it then. But now—"

"Did you tell the detective about the calls during the initial investigation?" Rick asked.

"No, it didn't seem important." The rapid-fire questions were getting her off-kilter.

Rick stared at her. "Do you know anyone in Alpine?"

She fidgeted and looked at the floor. "My cousin Tonia lived there then."

"You said Tonia was with whoever was in the barn that night," Brendan said. "Did she actually bring them in, or did you see her waiting in the truck? What was the sequence of events?"

"There was a black crew cab parked on the far side of the barn that night. As I told you, I'd fallen asleep and heard something. When I looked out the window, I saw Tonia in the backseat and a man in the front seat. She was pointing at the barn and saying something. Then she sat back and smiled." Lauren twisted her hands together.

Brendan nodded. "And then you turned around and saw another man in the barn with the needle. And Windsor dead."

"Two days later Tonia told the detective she saw me let a man into the barn, so of course I became a suspect."

"She was there too." Brendan said. "Wasn't she also a suspect?"

Lauren looked down at her hands. "She told them she'd come by to, um, have a talk with me."

Rick frowned. "What else aren't you saying?"

She glanced at Brendan, and he nodded to encourage her. "She thought I was trying to steal her boyfriend." She gripped her hands together. "I thought he was kind of repulsive, but he kept calling me and hanging around. She's married to him now, so I thought she'd be over it and maybe she would tell the truth. I called her last night, and she won't budge."

He would have to speak to this cousin.

~ette~

Lauren paused from training the young horse and wiped her brow. A red pickup rolled up the driveway, and she ducked through the corral fence and headed in its direction in case the occupants needed help figuring out where to go. Allie and Rick had gone to Betsy's school Christmas play, and none of the other employees were close by.

As she neared, she recognized the couple. When they stepped out of the truck, she hailed them. "Gary, Katrina! What a surprise, seeing you here!"

Gary turned at her voice and grinned. About forty, he reminded her of a squirrel with his round cheeks and dark eyes. He always had a ready smile too. They'd met at one of Tonia's parties and had hit it off immediately. His wife had been lonely and had found Lauren to be a soul mate. Lauren had gone out to dinner with him and his wife, Katrina, a couple of times in Fort Worth.

Katrina had her blond hair in a sleek new bob. She was tall and leggy with an easy manner. She hugged Lauren. "Lauren! What are you doing here?"

Lauren embraced her, then stepped back. "I'm working here now."

Katrina gasped and looked toward the ranch house. "What a small world. You've met Carly then, I assume?"

Lauren blinked. "Carly?"

Katrina's eyes clouded. "We're her guardians." She looked at her husband, briefly, as if expecting dissent. "Her mother was my first cousin. We agreed to be her guardians when she was born. Of course we never imagined a tragedy like this."

"Oh I'm so sorry. As I understand it, her parents died in a fire."

Katrina nodded. "It was a terrible thing."

Gary interrupted. "Katrina and I never planned to have children, but when something like this happens, well, it's not like you have a choice."

"Right, so we took her in. It hasn't been easy, I'll tell you that much. When she quit smiling and seemed so sad, I remembered how you'd raved about this place and how much it had helped you. I'd hoped it would do the same for her." She glanced toward the house. "Is she around?"

"Yes, she's with the other children in the bunkhouse at the back of the property. I'll call for her to come up." She pulled out her cell phone and called the house mother to send Carly up. "She'll be right here. Did she know you were coming?"

Gary shook his head. "I had to go to Alpine on business, and we decided we'd shoot down here for a brief visit."

The screen door banged, and Lauren's pulse jumped at the sight of Brendan's broad shoulders. He smiled at their visitors and headed to greet them. His limp was a little more pronounced this morning. Had he been neglecting his physical therapy?

"Hi, folks." He held out his hand. "Brendan Waddell."

Gary took his hand and introduced himself and his wife. "We're Carly's guardians."

Brendan looked them over. "We're pretty fond of that little girl. Lauren here has made it her quest to get her to laugh."

Katrina clasped her hands together. "I hope you can. I've tried everything."

Brendan leaned against the truck fender. "Anything special she's crazy about? A special doll, stuffed animal, anything?"

Gary shrugged. "Katrina's bought her everything you can imagine, but it's no use. She just goes back to sitting on her bed staring into the corner."

"Well, she's improved a bit then," Lauren said. "She's made

a good friend here, and she's participating in the activities. I'm going to give her a riding lesson this afternoon, her first."

The wind was picking up. Katrina pushed her hair out of her face. "Good luck with that. I tried taking her to a riding stable, and she was afraid of the horse."

Brendan looked at the path from the bunkhouses. "Here she comes now."

Carly's head was down as she walked toward the driveway. Dressed in white shorts and a red top, she scuffed her feet along the path. Lauren would give anything to see her skipping along like a normal five-year-old.

Katrina waved. "Carly!"

Carly's head jerked up, and she stared at the truck. Her pace only picked up a little until she stood before her guardians. She stood with her arms stiffly at her side as Katrina embraced her. "Do I have to leave now?"

Katrina's arms fell away and she stepped back. "No, honey, we just stopped to see how you are."

She released her clenched fists. "I like it here."

"I'm glad." Katrina started to touch Carly's head, then her hand dropped to her side. "But you have to come home sooner or later, you know. The kitty misses you."

"I don't like cats. I like dogs."

Lauren saw the helplessness on Katrina's face and jumped in to help. "You're doing well here though, aren't you, Carly?"

Her face brightened a bit, and she nodded. "I have a new bestest friend. Her name is Summer. She's six."

Gary touched the top of Carly's head. "That's nice, honey. Is there anything we can get for you? Anything you need?" Carly shook her head. Gary looked at her, then at his wife. "Okay, then. I guess we'll head on to my meeting. Call us if you need anything. Or even just to say hi. You haven't used your cell phone at all."

A cell phone for a child this small? Lauren stared at Gary a moment, then stepped back as he and Katrina got in the car. They were obviously trying, but they didn't seem to know how to relate to Carly. Lauren waved as they backed down the drive.

"Can I go back to play now?" Carly asked.

"Sure. Were you glad to see them?" Carly didn't answer, so Lauren touched her on the shoulder. "Go on back." She watched her run off with more eagerness than she'd shown coming their direction.

"What if I got her a puppy for Christmas?" Brendan asked. "She said she liked dogs. A dog can heal all kinds of emotional pain."

Lauren watched Carly disappear around the side of the house. "Maybe."

FIVE

BRENDAN HAD ALWAYS LIKED THE TOWN OF FORT STOCKTON, Texas. Cradled between the Davis Mountains and the Chihuahuan Desert, the area had a natural beauty that drew him. The town itself was a quaint and welcoming community with Old West storefronts and friendly people.

He could sense Lauren's tension in the passenger seat of his black Dodge pickup.

He pulled into the parking lot of a Piggly Wiggly. "Do we just drive up to your cousin's house and ask her the questions again?"

"I think Steve might be the key. I haven't talked to him since the murder. Maybe he could get her to tell the truth. He's an attorney."

"Good plan. Point me in the right direction."

"His office is just across the street. We can leave the truck here." She shoved open her door and got out.

He turned off the truck and jumped out too. Pain shot up his leg, and he resisted the urge to wince.

Lauren reversed direction and came to stand beside him. "What's wrong? Your leg?"

Though it was ludicrous, it bugged him that she'd noticed his weakness. "Just a twinge."

"It was a two-hour drive. We should have stopped along the way and let you exercise it. Did you do your physical therapy before we got started?"

He grinned to lighten the tension he felt. "Where'd you get your license, Doctor?"

Her full lips tipped up. "The school of equine injuries. I know a lot about this stuff, Brendan. I've got some liniment that would help it heal faster."

"It probably smells like cow dung."

She laughed then, a chuckle that grew from her belly into a sound that made his smile broaden. He liked the way she made him feel, the way she made him pause and pay attention. How did she do that?

He took her arm. "Let's go beard the tiger in his den."

She made a face. "He's not much of a tiger. More like a muskrat. He's not a man who makes most women take a second look to see if the muscles are real, like you."

Was that how she thought of him? It made him want to run to the nearest gym and pump up. The skin of her arm under his fingers was as smooth and soft as a new blade of grass. He caught a whiff of something sweet from her hair. His stomach rumbled. It was already nearly lunchtime. After they talked to the creep, maybe they could grab some food, and he could pry more of her personal life from her.

A historical plate on the front of the brick building proclaimed it had been built in 1897. The gray-green window trim added a tasteful bit of color, and the place had been well maintained. The painted sign in green and red listed Steve McAvoy as the only attorney inside. When he held open the door for Lauren, Brendan saw a man standing in the hall. His only concession to attorney-like attire was a string tie. His cowboy boots were well polished, and his shirt held sharp creases on the arms. About thirty, his blond hair was already balding in front. He was thin, almost gaunt.

His expression changed when his gaze fell on Lauren. His mouth dropped open, and he glanced behind him down the hall before taking two steps toward them. "Lauren, what are you doing here?" His voice was hushed, and he glanced behind him again.

Her smile was cordial. "Hello, Steve, I hope we're not bothering you."

"Um, actually, I was about to go out for lunch. Maybe you could come back this afternoon."

Brendan stepped between him and Lauren. "This won't take long. I wanted to ask you about the night Dustin Windsor died."

"I'm afraid I can't help you. I wasn't there."

"Where was Tonia that night?"

McAvoy wet his lips. "Who are you, anyway?"

"Brendan Waddell, Special Ops Intel." He tossed out his title in hopes of impressing McAvoy, but he should have known better. His military affiliation held no power with a senator.

43

"I fail to see what interest you have in this."

"I'm trying to help Lauren."

McAvoy's eyes narrowed, and he clenched his fists. "You're dating her?"

"No, just helping to clear her name."

The anger in the man seemed to ease. "Well, I'm afraid I can't help you. I know nothing about it."

"Steve?" High heels clicked on the tile floors, and an attractive redhead with a sprinkling of freckles appeared. Her gaze flickered to Lauren and she gaped. "You've got some nerve coming here."

McAvoy moved to intercept her. "They were just going, Tonia."

"What did you tell them?"

"There was nothing *to* tell."

The woman smiled then, but it didn't reach her eyes. "Of course not. Well, your little fishing expedition didn't net you anything, Lauren. I think the sheriff might be interested in speaking with you though. I'll give him a call." She turned and reached for the phone on the desk behind her.

In two steps, Brendan ripped it from her hand. "I don't think so. I'd like to know why you're so bent on sending your own cousin to jail. Afraid the detective will begin to look elsewhere? Like at you?"

Red bloomed in her cheeks. "Of course not." She folded her arms across her chest. "You can't stop me from calling the sheriff forever, you know. The minute you walk out that door, I'll have him on the phone."

"Why are you doing this to me?" Lauren asked, her throat tight. "I've always thought of you like a sister."

"You mean like a stepsister. You always got the best of everything, and I got the leftovers." Tonia lifted her chin. "Well, not this time. You're going to get what you deserve."

McAvoy put his hand on her shoulder. "Calm down, honey."

She shook off his grip. "You're so clueless, Steve. She would take everything from me if she could."

Lauren reached a shaking hand toward her cousin. "I hate this division between us. I don't know what to do about it. I still love you, Tonia."

Livid spots of red bloomed in Tonia's face. "Love, hah! If you'd loved me, you wouldn't have tried to seduce Steve. He told me all about it, so don't try to deny it."

Brendan glanced over to see Steve's face turn nearly purple. The lies in here were getting as deep as that cow dung he'd joked about. "Let's go, Lauren. We're getting nowhere here."

He took her arm and walked with her from the building.

The Mexican restaurant in Alpine looked almost like a house and had a horseshoe hung on the door. Lauren still felt shaken, so she asked the hostess for as much privacy as they could get.

"Cool," Brendan said when the hostess led them through the cowboy-decor room.

The walls were mottled in warm browns and tans, and the

doorway trim was terra-cotta. The hostess took them through the restaurant to the patio. Large cowboy murals decorated the side of the building. They were seated at a secluded table under a trellis on the patio. Grasses and yucca softened the surrounding buildings, and covered with twinkling lights, they made a holiday oasis outside.

He pulled a chair out for her, then settled beside her. "You okay? You're a little pale."

"I'm all right." She drew in a shaky breath. "Wow, she hates me. I don't know what to do with that."

"Has your relationship always been rocky?"

She shrugged. "It's had its ups and downs. She's bipolar so sometimes you never know which Tonia you're going to get. She takes a slight and magnifies it to proportions as big as a mountain. It's like she's just—snapped. Something pushed her over the edge with me." She kept seeing the expression on her cousin's face as she spewed out vitriol.

"Did you see how he acted when he thought we might be dating? He's married to your cousin, but he still has the hots for you. He could be dangerous."

Dangerous? She'd never liked Steve, but he'd never frightened her. On the other hand, Tonia had scared her today. Lauren blinked her stinging eyes. "Betrayal is hard to handle. I never would have dreamed Tonia could do something like this, but she still seems determined to see me in jail. She was ready to call the sheriff."

"Yeah, but it was all bluff. She lives here. Her lies would find her out if she dragged in the local guys."

"But you hightailed it out of Fort Stockton before stopping for lunch."

"No sense in taking a chance. But yeah, I don't think she made a call when we left. I bet she gave old Steve an earful though."

The server came to take their order, and as soon as she left them alone, Brendan leaned back in his chair and stared at her. "I want to know more about the history between the two of you. Your mom raised her until she died when you were fifteen."

Heat ran up her cheeks. "You've checked me out."

He shrugged. "It's what I do best. After your mom died, you were in the same foster home, correct?"

She shook her head. "Actually, we were in different homes. We got to go to the same high school at least, but it was never the same. Tonia got picked on a lot. I got to look after her at school."

"So you mothered her too."

Her pulse skipped at the expression in his warm eyes. "Too?"

"You mother everyone. Carly, for example." His smile broadened. "And threatening to doctor me with some vile-smelling liniment."

She couldn't hold back a smile. "Older sisters tend to do that."

"You have any other siblings?"

"Just Tonia, and well, you know about that relationship."

"I'm sorry you had to go through that. No wonder you are so good with those kids. It doesn't seem fair you ended up having such trouble on top of trouble." He picked up his fork and ran it through his fingers. "I think either Steve or Tonia know who killed Dusty Windsor."

"Why?"

He tapped the end of his nose. "It smells to high heaven. She gains nothing by throwing suspicion on you unless she's afraid of something. I think it's more than fear of losing her man, or even fear of having the police look at her too closely. What are her habits? She have any expensive hobbies?"

She reached for a tortilla chip and scooped up some salsa. The burn stayed on her tongue. "She likes to travel. She makes two trips out West every year. Says it clears her head. She asked to borrow some money for a trip about a month before all this happened."

"Out West, huh? Where out West?"

"Nevada, mostly. She likes to hike out there."

"Are you kidding me? Hiking in Nevada? Lauren, is Tonia a gambler?"

"What? No, I . . ." Lauren thought for a moment. It made sense.

"Did you give her the money?"

Hating to admit she'd been foolish, she began to tear her napkin into strips. "Yeah, I did. Two thousand dollars."

He whistled softly through his teeth. "You ever think about exercising some tough love and saying no?"

"All the time." She heaved a heavy sigh. "Sometimes it's just easier to give her what she wants."

"If Tonia is a gambler and is borrowing money, she could be in over her head."

"Does refinancing her house count? She was working on that just before the murder."

His eyes brightened. "I can check that out, see how much she got and if it sounded like she needed more."

The server brought their food, and her mouth watered at the wafting aroma of *arroz con polla*. Eating would keep her mind off how much she liked being with Brendan. His offer of help made her believe it just might come out all right. When had anyone last reached out to her with genuine concern? It had been a long time.

Six

AFTER SPENDING TIME WITH LAUREN, BRENDAN REALIZED HE believed in her innocence. While they waited for the check, he placed a call to one of his contacts and asked him to check on how much money Tonia got when she refinanced her house. And also to check out any trail where her finances might lead.

He left money on the table for the bill. "Ready? I told Rick we'd do some Christmas shopping for the kids."

She brightened. "For all those kids? How will we pay for it? I'm a little short since buying Angel from McLeod."

"No problem. I'll buy them and Rick can pay me back later."

"All right then. I love to shop. Especially for kids. Do you have a list?"

He pulled out a paper from his pocket and waved it in front of her. "It's a little daunting."

She grabbed it from his hand and scanned it. "It's not that bad. It will be fun buying dolls and fire trucks. What was your favorite toy as a child, Brendan?"

"G.I. Joe, of course." He grinned, remembering his collection of action figures.

"I bet you were always the hero sneaking in to rescue the prisoners."

He looked away from her intent stare. "I'm no hero."

"Sure you are." Her voice was soft. "I heard Rick telling the children you'd rescued ten guys in Afghanistan recently. I bet there are many more who owe their lives to you."

He shrugged. "It's just my job."

"Right."

The attention made him a little uncomfortable, but it felt, well, kind of good to see the admiration in her eyes. "My dad was a Marine, and I wanted to be just like him. It wasn't until I'd enlisted that I found out his dark side. He had a string of women. Mom covered it up well, but she knew all these years he had feet of clay. And he was a lousy dad with a hard fist."

"Is that why you've never married? You're afraid you'd be like him in that way too?"

He controlled his expression as he stared at the certainty in her eyes. "Maybe." He would never want to cause the kind of pain he saw in his mother. "My brother ended up just like him. Maybe I would too."

"You're a good man, Brendan. It didn't take me long to see that. Not many guys would go out of their way to help someone like me."

"Someone like you? What does that mean?"

"I'm nobody. No power or money. A foster kid who's had to fight for everything I've managed to accomplish in my life."

He smiled, drawn to everything about her. "The plucky underdog who never lets anything get her down. You're one of those who will come from behind to win the race because you never give up."

A smile spread across her face and lit her eyes. "Is that right? It sometimes feels like I'll never manage to put one foot in front of the other."

"But you keep going. I like that about you." In fact, he liked everything about her. The relentless way she clung to hope, the way she refused to be a victim. She would never stop fighting for her family, unlike his mother.

His words hung in the air, and a breathless charge permeated the air. The smile in her eyes nearly dazzled him, and he had an almost uncontrollable urge to lean down and brush his lips across hers, but he managed to check the impulse. He'd known her, what, two days? It felt like two years though. He'd never felt such an instant connection to someone. He'd heard of love at first sight, but he'd always thought it was baloney. Now he wasn't so sure.

Shields up. His mental command did little to quench the fire spreading through his limbs when he looked down at her parted lips. He finally tore his gaze away and nodded to the block of stores on the street. "Guess we'd better get started."

"I think so. We're still an hour and a half from home, and Allie is expecting us back for supper."

"She's a good woman. Rick is lucky to have her. In fact, Rick is lucky in a lot of ways. Living out here in all of God's beauty, working with horses. It seems so far from the life I've been living."

"Are you eager to go back?"

Her voice seemed a little husky, but he didn't dare think about what that might mean. He shook his head. "I would miss the excitement, but with this gimpy leg, I'm not sure what's waiting for me."

"Your limp is getting better."

"You sound like you're trying to get rid of me."

Her hand came down on his. "I'll hate it when you leave."

"I might not leave. I've been thinking about taking a medical discharge." Until the words came out of his mouth, he'd pushed away every thought leading in that direction. But now that he'd said it, it didn't seem so impossible.

Her fingers tightened on his. "What would you do?"

"I don't know. Help out Rick. Maybe adopt a passel of kids myself and see what kind of father I'd make." He cleared his throat and turned toward the storefronts. "Let's see if we can get everything at this general store. They probably have toys too." He held the door open for her and sniffed her sweet scent as she went by.

A clerk directed them to the two shelves of toys, but the store was well stocked with the types of items they needed. They quickly went down the list and filled their cart with an assortment of items that would be sure to bring smiles on Christmas morning. He whipped out his wallet and produced his debit card to pay for everything.

"That cost more than I expected," Lauren said when they walked out of the store with their bags.

"It wasn't bad."

"Oh, wait. We forgot to get a receipt. I'll run back in and get it so you can give it to Rick."

"Forget about it, and let's go."

She stopped and stared up at him. The brilliant sunshine illuminated the golden lights in her big brown eyes. "You're not going to let Rick repay you, are you?"

He squirmed under the beam of her admiration. "Nope. He spends every penny he has on those kids. It's the least I can do. I don't have anyone else to buy Christmas presents for." He took her arm and turned her back toward his truck.

She resisted the tug of his fingers. "Look, Brendan." She pointed to a sign in the window of a feed store. "Puppies!"

He studied the fat puppies. "You're thinking what I'm thinking? Allie might shoot us. And what about Carly's guardians? They might have something to say about her dragging a puppy home with her."

"They seem to want to do anything they can for her. I can talk them into it."

He couldn't resist the appeal in her eyes. "It's on your head then."

"I'll take the blame." Her smile turned radiant, and she rushed to the door.

He followed with a grin. Her childlike enthusiasm touched him. They approached the counter, and the middle-aged woman brightened when she heard they were interested in a puppy.

She gestured to a box at the end of the counter. "No one

has taken any of them yet, so you can have the pick of the litter."

Lauren knelt beside the box. "Oh, they are adorable! They look at least part golden retriever."

"Part golden and part Lab," the woman said.

He mentally groaned. "I was hoping for a small dog."

"Small dogs are yappy. There is no better dog than a golden or a Lab." Lauren scooped up a golden bundle of fur and held it to her cheek. "He's precious. We'll take him."

The woman shook her head. "He's the runt of the litter, and he has a little bit of a limp. Pick another one."

A gimpy leg, just like him. But with some love and care, that little pup would be running around.

Lauren shifted the puppy to one arm and opened her purse with the other. "Even better. He'll need a good home. How much?"

The woman shrugged. "The rest are a hundred, but I can let this one go for fifty."

Brendan took out a hundred dollar bill before Lauren could pull out her wallet. "He's worth the hundred."

He would have paid ten times that amount to bring that kind of glow to Lauren's face.

~∂℮~

It was going to be hard to hide the puppy for another week. The poor thing didn't leave Lauren's side, so she put him in her bed and turned out the light. He snuggled against her, and she rested her chin on top of his soft head.

What a lovely, lovely day. She liked Brendan entirely too much. Even her reckless heart recognized the danger. Before long, he'd recover from his injury and he'd be off on another adventure. She didn't want the kind of man who left her worried and anxious. What kind of life would that be? And he might die and leave her, just like Mom.

Even if he had feelings for her, and there were no guarantees about that, she was treading on dangerous ground. There seemed to be some kind of attraction between them, but her naïveté could lead her to read more into his intense glances than he intended. She wasn't a good judge of what men thought.

What if he is looking to add me to his conquests?

She rejected the thought immediately. He wasn't that kind of guy. Integrity resided in every cell of his body. She would bet her life on that. Besides, Rick and Allie adored him.

So what did those warm glances and the tension between them mean? And did she want it to lead to anything at all?

She inhaled the good scent of new puppy and closed her eyes only to open them at a sound outside her door. It might have only been one of the horses moving about, but something about the sliding, muffled noise sounded furtive. Maybe it was just Brendan coming to check on her and the puppy.

Cradling the little dog against her chest, she slipped out of bed and stepped to the door. She put her ear against the door but heard nothing. She opened it a crack and peered out. The inside of the barn was dark, illuminated in spots by the moon shining through the windows.

"Hello? Anyone there?"

A horse snuffled in answer, but there was no other sound. She shut the door and went back to her room. Her imagination again. She climbed back into bed and slid under the sheet. Her pulse finally slowed, and she closed her eyes. Her breathing slowed, and she began to drift toward sleep.

In her dream she was struggling with a dark figure in the bed who was choking her. She couldn't breathe. She slammed her hand against his head, and when her fingertips scratched against rough beard—This was no dream! Her eyes flew open, but it was too dark to make out more than a figure looming over her with his hands on her neck.

Gasping for air, she kicked the sheet away from her and shoved her hands upward. His fingers around her neck didn't budge. The puppy yapped as she struggled harder, and she felt him lunge away from her.

The man cursed, and the puppy yelped but didn't come back to her for shelter. She had to help him. Gathering the last of her air, she pulled her knees to her chest and shoved upward with her calves. The grip on her throat loosened, and he rocked back.

She rolled away and off the other side of the bed, reaching for the baseball bat she always kept in the corner. Her right hand closed around the handle, comforting in its solid feel.

The shadowy figure lunged at her, and she swung the bat at his head the way she would at a softball. There was a sound like a stick hitting a melon, and she felt the satisfying shudder in the bat all the way up to her shoulder. He was still standing though, and she thought he had his hand to his ear. The string of curses rolling out of his mouth could have turned the air blue.

She finally had enough air in her lungs to shriek. A long pent-up scream that didn't sound like it could come from her nearly pierced her ears.

He lunged toward her again. "You little—"

She turned and ran for the door, then stopped. Where was the puppy? Had he hurt the little guy? She ducked through the door and stood to one side with her heart pounding. Through the window she saw lights flicker to life in the big house. Brendan and Rick would be here any moment. It would be more sensible to wait on them, but what if that guy took out his rage on the puppy?

She lifted the bat to her shoulder and stepped into the center of the doorway. Reaching around to the side wall, she flipped on the light, then blinked. The room was empty, and a breeze lifted the curtains of the open window. She nearly sagged with relief, then rushed into the room. The puppy wasn't on the bed. She dropped to her knees and looked under the bed where she found the little mite cowering on his belly.

"Come here, boy." She waggled her fingers, and he scooted on his belly toward her, whimpering the whole way. She scooped him up and hugged his trembling body to her chest, then scrambled to her feet with adrenaline still shuddering through her body.

She turned at the sound of footsteps pounding toward her room. Brendan's panicked voice shouted her name, and she staggered toward the door to fall into his arms.

His strong embrace held her close, and she listened to the thud of his heart under her ear. It was a few moments before she found the strength to raise her head and tell him what happened.

When he tipped her chin up and examined the marks on her throat, his eyes went dark. "I'll find him."

SEVEN

SITTING ON THE SOFA BESIDE HER, BRENDAN DABBED SOME ointment on the angry welts standing out on Lauren's neck. He didn't know what to do with the rage that made his hands tremble a bit. The man had dared to come here on Bluebird property and attack her. He wanted to wrap his fingers around the thug's throat and give him a taste of what he'd put Lauren through.

He finished his ministrations. "Does it hurt much?"

"Not too badly." Her voice sounded hoarse.

"I think you'll have some trouble talking tomorrow. Rest your voice as much as you can. I think you need to see a doctor."

She shifted away and shook her head. "I'll be all right."

Allie came in carrying a tray with a teapot and cups. "I thought the warm tea might help your throat, Lauren. You want sugar in it?" She set the tray on the table and poured a cup of tea, then handed it to Lauren who fumbled with it a little.

"Sorry, my hands are cold. I'll just have a dollop of cream too."

Allie glanced at Rick. "Would you start a fire, honey? Her hands are cold."

She touched her throat. "I thought I was dreaming at first."

Rick knelt in front of the woodstove and began to load it with wood. "Did you get a look at him?" He held a match to the paper, and it blackened, then burst into flames. The wood caught and he closed the door.

Lauren shook her head. "It was too dark. The puppy tried to bite him. It distracted him enough that I was able to fight back."

Brendan's fingers found the soft fur of the puppy curled up on his lap. "Thank God for this little guy." He couldn't mask the fervency in his voice. What if that creep had killed her? The thought made him shudder. "He seems okay."

"I think the man knocked him to the floor. He yelped." She scooted closer and reached over to rub the puppy's head.

The warmth emanating from her made him want to move closer and put his arm around her. He stayed where he was and kept his gaze on the little dog.

She took a sip of her tea and grimaced. "Hurts."

Allie headed back toward the kitchen. "I'll get you some ibuprofen."

Rick sat in the chair opposite them. "Did the guy say anything?"

"Nothing but curses when I hit him with the baseball bat." She looked up at Brendan. "But there was something about the shape of him and the timbre of his voice. I think it was the same guy who killed Dustin. I could be wrong, but I don't think so."

Brendan processed the information and logically began to connect the dots. "How could he have tracked you here? No one knows where you are."

"Tonia knows." She bit her lip. "She could have tracked me here with the phone I used. She's the only one I've called."

"I'm going to see if there's any answer to my query about her." Brendan reached for his laptop on the side table and opened it, then navigated to his e-mail. "Yeah, looks like I have a response." He opened the message and scanned it. "Looks like Tonia owed everyone and their brother. She got twenty grand on her refi, tried to get a second mortgage, but was turned down. She opened a high-interest rate credit card and took an advance immediately. That money went to a casino in Oklahoma."

Lauren's arm brushed his. "What's the situation now?"

"All her debt was wiped out. She doesn't owe anything but a small payment on her car."

"When did the payoff happen?"

He scanned the screen, and his gut clenched. "When was the murder?"

"Two months ago."

He turned his head to stare at her. "She paid all that debt off on October 15."

Her eyes dilated and she inhaled. "Less then two weeks later."

Coldness settled over him at the desolation in her voice. Betrayal like this shouldn't happen in families. "I think we need to have another talk with your cousin. When did she marry McAvoy?"

"I don't know. Maybe Steve helped her with those debts."

He turned back to his keyboard. "Should be a matter of public record." He logged into the right website and began to peruse. "A month later, November 15. So it didn't take her long to drag him to the altar once you were out of the picture."

Allie returned with a bottle of ibuprofen. "Let's not jump to conclusions. Could McAvoy have given her the money?"

"The report doesn't say where the source of the money came from. I'll have it looked into. It might take a couple of days to track that down."

"Steve isn't poor, but I don't know if he'd have that kind of money sitting around. A lot of people, even professionals, live on everything they make and don't stick money in savings."

He grinned. "Which brings up another area of research. Let's see what we can find out about McAvoy's finances too." He sent off a request for a report on the attorney.

The weight of her gaze on him was like a rock. He glanced up and lifted a brow. "What?"

Color touched her cheeks, and she looked down at her hands. "You're pretty impressive, Brendan. Overwhelmingly so."

He quickly looked away before his expression gave away how much her words touched him.

⁂

Lauren touched her hand to her sore throat. "You didn't have to walk me back to my room." The crisp air felt good on her overheated skin. Just being near Brendan did erratic things to her temperature. She inhaled. "The air smells good. I love sage. There's nothing like it." The puppy scampered around her feet, nipping at insects in the dirt.

Brendan stopped outside the barn door. "I'm not just walking you home. I'm going to sleep in the hay. Rick had one of the hands bring over a sleeping bag for me."

The moonlight illuminated his face. His lips were pressed together and his gaze held serious intent. This wasn't a man who ran away from anything. She'd never felt so protected, not even when she was a kid. Her mother had tried, but after her dad had died, life held an edge of danger to her. There was never enough money, often not enough food. They moved from rental house to rental house, and she lived in fear of a hard knock on the door as an owner evicted them, and they had to find another place to live.

"Thank you." Her voice was a husky whisper. "I was a little scared to go back to my room, even though I knew Rick had two men staked out here."

His teeth glimmered in the bit of light as he smiled. "Allie offered you a bed in the house."

"I didn't want you to think I was a weakling. Not after that speech about me being an underdog who never quits. I didn't want to be a quitter."

His fingers, firm yet gentle, touched her under the chin and tipped her head up. "There's no quitting spirit in you."

His eyes smoldered with an intense emotion she was afraid

to name. What if she was misjudging this attraction between them? She didn't want to make a fool of herself. The man was a heartbreaker if she'd ever seen one. Not that he would intend to hurt her, but she was more fragile than he knew. Her heart had never been tried like this. There'd only been casual flirtations over the years. He tempted her in ways she wasn't willing to admit.

"I'm not going to let anyone hurt you."

"Not even you?" The words were out before she could call them back. She stepped away and turned toward the door, but he caught her arm and gently rotated her back to face him.

He brushed the hair away from her face.

A bubble of laughter welled in her chest, and she let out a nervous chuckle.

"I would never hurt you. We both feel it, Lauren. There's a deep attraction between us. I don't know where it came from, but I'm not going to lie. You are the most beautiful, intriguing woman I've ever met."

Her throat felt even tighter. *"Beautiful . . . intriguing."* No one had ever said that about her. She was just . . . Lauren. A horse-crazy woman in a heap of trouble. She usually felt anything but special, but with his gaze boring through to her innermost thoughts, she could have sworn she'd grown two inches and was on the cover of *Mademoiselle*.

"Why is this happening? I've never believed in . . ." She wasn't about to say the word.

His hand touching her hair moved to cup her cheek. "Love at first sight?"

She barely nodded. Was this love? Could it happen that fast? It had to be major attraction, not love. But something in her soul wanted to know his innermost thoughts, his dreams, his desires. Events were swirling so fast around them, and maybe that was why everything felt so ramped up.

His thumb stroked her cheek, and her insides turned to mush. She couldn't think past the feel of his fingertips gliding along her face. Her eyelids fluttered shut, and she leaned in, inhaling his musky male scent and the spicy aroma of his cologne.

His hand slid to the back of her head, and his lips came down on hers with a tender, yet insistent pressure. She wrapped both arms around his neck and kissed him back with everything in her. The scrape of his faint whiskers against her face rooted her in the moment. Lauren wished it could last forever. She'd never experienced a kiss that swept her along on a tidal wave of emotion like this one.

She was still clinging to him when he pulled away and gave a shaky laugh. "I think I'd better get you inside, or I might not let you go."

Her heart still hammered against her ribs as she stumbled into the barn to her bedroom door. She felt as though she'd just lived through some kind of explosion. She paused outside her door. "Good night."

He still hadn't released her arm. "I'll be right outside if you need me."

"I know." She couldn't seem to make her hand open the door. "Um, could we try just one more kiss?"

His only answer was to draw her into his arms again. This kiss was even more shattering to her sanity than the last one. She gave herself over to the emotions racing through her and clung to him like a rider on a wild horse. She knew only the feel of his mouth on hers and the taste of him on her lips. She caught the last shred of sanity and pulled away so the brush of night air could cool her heated cheeks.

"You sure make it hard to say good night." His voice was a low rumble, and he dropped his hand from her arm.

"I think you're right." Her fingers seemed to find their strength, and she twisted the knob and practically fell into the room. The puppy dashed in past her feet and turned to look at her as if to ask if she was coming.

"Everything look okay?"

She spared a glance around. "Yes. Good night." She shut the door before she gave in to the temptation to kiss him again.

EIGHT

BRENDAN BUTTONED HIS RED SHIRT. HE COULDN'T REMEMBER the last time he'd been this excited about Christmas, which brought him up short. Shouldn't the day of Jesus Christ's birth always be holy and special to him? And yet something about this one had his senses heightened and his hope buoyed. The yard was empty and dark as he strode toward the twinkling Christmas lights on the big house.

The children were chatting excitedly when he joined everyone else in the large living room. Several of the parents were there as well. He nodded at Gary and Katrina Foreshaw on one of the sofas. Had Lauren told them they were about to get a puppy at their house? The kids sat in a circle around the glimmering Christmas tree heaped with packages. The scent of pine permeated the air and mingled with the tangible excitement wafting off the children.

He settled into an armchair to the left of the tree. His gaze shot over to collide with Lauren's. He'd barely slept last night, jolting awake every time one of the horses snorted. The evening had passed uneventfully though, and he was thankful for that.

Allie and Rick had opted to let the children open gifts now since so many were leaving tonight to spend Christmas with their families. The puppy had been stashed in Rick and Allie's bedroom, and Brendan kept thinking he could hear it whine, but maybe it was his imagination.

A children's Bible in hand, Rick moved to the Christmas tree. "How many have heard the Christmas story?"

Only two children held up their hands. Carly wasn't one of them, and Brendan frowned. Wouldn't all children have heard this at least once? The children quieted as Rick began to read Matthew's account of the birth of Jesus. The children's eyes were wide and intent as they listened.

Rick finished the story and closed the Bible. "So that's why we celebrate Christmas. It's Jesus' birthday, and we give gifts to people we love, to share his love. He loves each of you very much, and so do we."

Allie led the children in "Silent Night," and several of them didn't sing until the second chorus when they joined in hesitantly.

Rick set the Bible on the stand by Brendan, then turned to the tree. "So let's distribute the presents. Brendan, could you help me?"

Brendan rose and handed out packages. The room turned loud with children squealing and talking excitedly. Soon the room was awash in brightly colored paper and empty boxes as the kids hugged their gifts to their chests.

Carly sat on the floor to one side with Summer. All she'd gotten so far was a small doll, but she didn't seem to notice she hadn't gotten as much as the other children. He glanced at Lauren and signaled her to go get the puppy.

Her cheeks pink, she got up and hurried from the room. He stepped closer to Carly and put his hand on her head. "Carly, we have a special surprise for you."

Carly glanced up, her green eyes wide. She still didn't seem to grasp the gift might be hers. Lauren entered the room with the puppy in her hands. The little fur ball yipped, and Carly's gaze shot over to Lauren. She didn't rise though. Poor kid had probably lost all ability to hope for good things in her life.

The children were talking excitedly, and Brendan held up his hand. "Quiet, kids. We can't even think."

Lauren put the puppy on the floor, and its little belly practically rubbed the ground. The puppy pounced on a roll of red wrapping paper, and the children giggled. An entranced expression on her face, Carly scooted slightly closer to the puppy and reached out her hand. The puppy sauntered closer and sniffed her fingers. She stroked his head.

Lauren squatted in front of her. "It's a boy puppy. What's his name?

Carly glanced up. "He's your puppy. You should know his name."

"Carly, he's not my puppy. He's yours. Merry Christmas."

The little girl's mouth gaped. Her gaze darted to Brendan's, then back to the puppy. "Mine?" She tipped her head to the side, eyebrows raised.

Lauren nodded. "Yes, we bought him for you. Me and Mr. Brendan."

Carly's lips trembled, and her eyes glistened with moisture. "Why would you do that?"

"He needed you. And you needed him."

Carly reached over and slid her hand under the puppy's belly, then lifted him onto her lap. He wriggled all over and stretched up to lick her chin. Her eyes widened, and a small giggle escaped her lips. She looked up at the Foreshaws. "Can I keep him?"

Gary's smile was pinched. "I don't think we have a choice."

A smile—the first Brendan had seen on her face—lifted Carly's lips. His heart kicked in his chest to see that smile. They'd worked so hard for it. Without consciously thinking about it, he took Lauren's hand and helped her rise. They stood there, hand in hand, as Carly held the puppy and kissed his soft, furry head. The puppy snuggled closer and tucked his head under her arm. After pushing half his neck under her arm as well, he went still.

"He's the runt of the litter, and the owner even tried to talk me out of buying him," Lauren said. "It's hard to be unwanted."

"I want him!" Carly's face was radiant. "And he wants me."

"We thought so too," Brendan said. "That's why we had to get him. We knew he would fit your lap perfectly."

The other children crowded around, and Carly allowed them to touch her dog before getting up with the puppy in her arms. "I know his name!" She clutched him more tightly, and he wiggled and whined until she set him back on the floor. "His name is Tucker. That's the road I lived on with my mommy and daddy." The puppy pounced on a ball of paper and gave a tiny bark as if to say he approved of his name. "He likes it!"

Lauren's fingers tightened around Brendan's, and her eyes glistened with tears when she glanced up at him. *Thank you*, she mouthed.

He smiled and squeezed her fingers. "You're the one who picked him out. Good choice. I think we hit this one out of the park."

"I think so too."

Something about her voice made him stare at her. "You okay?"

She nodded, her gaze on the little girl and puppy. "I just remembered something. Carly said they lived on Tucker Road. The fire that killed Carly's parents must've been the same night Dustin died. I saw the blaze in the distance. I think the sirens on the fire truck were what woke me. I never made the connection until now. I didn't realize *that* fire was the one that killed her parents."

He squeezed her fingers again. "No wonder you and Carly seem connected."

Her gaze wandered over to the Foreshaws then back to Carly. "Poor little girl."

ɔℓℓ

Once the children trooped off to bed, Lauren caught Brendan's eye, and they said their good nights to the rest of the adults. Out on the porch, the cool night breeze lifted her hair and cooled her heated cheeks. She didn't want to examine her suspicions too closely, but she had to.

She gestured to the swing under the big cottonwood tree. "Let's sit there."

"It's nearly freezing, and you don't have a coat." But he sat on the swing and scooted over.

"I'm not cold. Not yet." She settled on the wooden swing and gave a push with her feet. The chain creaked on the limb overhead as she settled back against the swing. The spicy scent of his cologne mingled with the aroma of creosote and sage.

"What's wrong? You haven't been yourself since you told me you needed to talk to me."

"I remembered something I saw the night Dustin died."

"In the barn?"

She shook her head. "Remember I told you I'd been sleeping and something woke me? I thought it was probably the truck outside, the one Tonia was in. But I don't think it was that at all. I got up and looked out the window. I'd been focused on the truck Tonia was in, but I didn't pay attention to the other truck. Not until tonight."

He sat up straight. "What other truck?"

"There was a truck that went by on the road. I saw the dust from its tires as it turned off Tucker Road."

He went silent a moment. "Tucker Road. The road Carly mentioned?"

She nodded. At least she didn't have to explain her line of thinking. He was tracking with her. "I'd seen that truck plenty of times. It was Gary Foreshaw's truck. But why would he be driving *away* from the fire? Wouldn't he try to help? After all, Mrs. Jacobsen was Katrina's cousin."

"I'm not sure what you're saying here. You're not accusing Foreshaw of something, are you?"

She rubbed her forehead. The days had been so confusing and upsetting. "I've known the Foreshaw's awhile. Gary is big into gambling on the races. The Jacobsen's had one of the best racing stables around. It's probably nothing, but . . ."

"But it looks suspicious." He pulled out his phone. "Let me check on something." He rose and walked a few feet away.

Lauren watched him pace in the moonlight and listened to the soothing cadence of his deep voice. So this was what it felt like to be able to rely on someone else, to be at peace without waves of fear battering at her.

She closed her eyes and listened to the night sounds spring to life around her. God's creation in all its diversity. Calm settled over her soul. Things were going to be all right. God had sent someone to come alongside her, to help her out of the mess she'd been in.

She could hardly believe how much her life had changed.

Brendan returned to drop onto the swing beside her. "All the Jacobsen assets passed into the Foreshaws' hands since Katrina was the only blood relative. He has been taking his horses to every race in the country. With a little research, we can find out how many of those races have had unexplained injuries to jockeys or horses. I should know something tomorrow."

She absorbed the news in silence. "Did you find out anything about the fire that killed Carly's parents?"

He nodded, his gaze never leaving her. "They've ruled it suspicious. They found traces of an accelerant in the kitchen."

"Have they talked to Gary and Katrina?"

"Yeah. They have an alibi. They were out to dinner with friends and didn't get home until after ten. Friends corroborated their story."

She clutched his hand. "But I saw him that night. It was about eight."

His fingers tightened around hers. "I think it's suspicious. You need to tell the police what you saw."

Her stomach plunged, and she felt dizzy at the thought of facing the judgment in their eyes. "Oh, Brendan, they won't even believe me."

"They can check it out more, put some pressure on the couple who gave them the alibi." His fingers brushed her chin and he tipped her face up toward his. "I know it will be hard, honey, but it's time to quit running. Time to find a calm center to deal with all this."

"Funny you should mention that. I was just thinking how peaceful and calm it felt here tonight." She looked toward the house where the Christmas lights still twinkled. "What a perfect season to search for peace."

NINE

Tucker Road.

The words played over and over in Lauren's head as she walked back to her room to grab her sweater. Could she be right about her suspicions? She hated to suspect anyone, especially Carly's guardian. The whole thing tied her up in knots.

She slipped her arms into her sweater as the wind swirled around the side of the barn and poked cold fingers against her skin. When she entered the barn, she paused a moment to get her bearings in the dim wash of light from a single bulb. Angel snorted a greeting, but he seemed skittish, tossing his head when she took a step in his direction. Something felt off, and she turned back toward the door. No sense in taking any chances.

Her hand on the door, she heard a sliding sound. A figure stepped from the shadows on the other side of Angel's stall.

Gary Foreshaw wore an easy smile. "Hey, Lauren. I wanted to talk to you a second."

She glanced behind him. "Where's Katrina?"

"She took Carly to town for a little shopping before we head out."

"It's a little late, Gary. What did you want to talk about?" She kept her tone brisk and her hand on the door. His presence here might be a confirmation of her suspicions.

He shoved his hands in his pockets and stepped nearer. For a moment he didn't speak but stared into her face. "You figured it out, didn't you?"

Her stomach plunged, and her fingers tightened on the door handle. "Figured what out?" She should shove open the door and escape, but she had to know the truth.

"Don't play games, Lauren. I saw it on your face when Carly named the puppy."

"You started the fire at the Jacobsen's. I didn't remember seeing your truck leaving when the fire was raging until tonight. Dustin's death seemed more pressing."

He nodded. "I always figured you'd eventually remember."

She tipped her chin up. "But how could you? They were your family. Katrina's family, anyway. Why would you kill them in such a horrific way?"

"They were already dead when I set fire to the house. I'm not a monster, you know. Besides, I'd hardly call them family. You don't shut out your family. You don't rob family blind like he did me."

Had he moved slightly closer? She couldn't quite tell in the dim light. The smart thing would be to leave right now. Or scream. "So it was all about money?"

He shrugged. "What else? I could have lost everything. I had no choice. Surely you can see that."

Listening to his voice detailing all the "reasons" turned her stomach. "Tonia helped you, didn't she? And in return you helped her get out of debt."

His eyes widened. "You're smart, Lauren. Too smart."

She didn't have time to react before he grabbed her arm in a steely grip. His other hand came out of his pocket with a bandana. She twisted away from the sweet chemical scent and opened her mouth to scream.

Before she could make a sound, he stuffed the handkerchief in her mouth and held it over her nose. She coughed, and her vision blurred as she inhaled the sickly odor. No matter how hard she pulled, she couldn't get her arm out of his grip.

Her knees gave way, and she started to sink to the floor in spite of squeezing the handle with one hand and being supported by Gary with the other. She released her hold on the door and yanked at his hand as he loosened his pressure on the cloth in order to keep her from falling.

She managed to twist away from the handkerchief and took a wonderful breath of hay-scented air before he moved the cloth back into place.

The rough wooden boards under her hands anchored her at the floor. She rolled away from his control, but the pressure on her face didn't ease, though she managed to get onto her back. She kicked up but it was a feeble attempt at freedom.

The last thing she saw was his vile smile.

Brendan glanced out his bedroom window and frowned. Lauren wasn't back yet, and it shouldn't take this long to get her sweater. Her bedroom light had never gone on. Was something wrong with one of the horses? He shoved his feet into flip-flops and ran for the barn.

The yard was quiet except for the skitters and chirps of night insects and animals as he hurried toward the barn. He caught his breath when he neared the building. The door stood open. A faintly sweet odor hung in the air, and he instantly recognized it as ether. His throat tightened, and he curled his hands into fists.

He should have brought his gun. Poking his head into the barn, he glanced around. "Lauren?" He didn't expect an answer, not with that smell hanging around.

Her horse tossed his head and snorted, obviously agitated. Brendan strode to the stall and looked in to make sure she wasn't lying on the floor. Nothing but hay.

Someone has taken her.

Though his first reaction was to hit something, his instincts kicked in. His cell phone was still in his jean pocket so he pulled it out and called the sheriff's office. Had her cousin taken her? Or whoever killed Windsor?

He asked the sheriff to put out a BOLO on her, and the sheriff said he'd get right on it. The "Be On the Lookout" order probably wouldn't get him anywhere in this remote part of Texas. Traffic was light around here at any time, and he wasn't about to depend on a sighting to find the woman he loved. The thought made him stumble before he caught himself.

He got to work examining the barn. There had been a scuffle right here by the door. The odor was strongest here too. She hadn't been gone long or the smell would have dissipated. He followed drag marks out the door and around the side of the barn to where a vehicle had been parked. A truck, by the looks of the tracks.

He knelt and studied the footprints. About a man's size eleven. The light on the end of the barn glinted off something in the weeds. A cell phone. He scooped it up and swiped it on. Lauren's phone.

But who had taken her? He rose and stared into the dark night. He had to find her before it was too late, and there was only one person who might know. He navigated to Lauren's address book and found her cousin's number. As the call rang through, he strode back toward the house to wake Rick.

The phone clicked on the other end, and Tonia's irritated voice blared in his ear. "Lauren, I told you not to call me. Do you realize how late it is?"

"This isn't Lauren. This is Brendan Waddell. Your cousin has been abducted, and you're going to tell me who has her or I'll have your butt hauled into jail."

A soft gasp came through the phone. "Abducted? How do you know? Maybe she just went for a ride or something."

"I found the signs of a scuffle and smelled ether. Someone dragged her out of the barn and to a waiting truck. Her phone was in the weeds. That enough to convince you she's in mortal danger?"

A muted man's voice asked who she was talking to and she answered him. "It's that friend of Lauren's. She's missing."

Could it be Tonia's husband? He'd been obsessed with Lauren. Maybe he'd snapped and taken her. The voice might be another man. If McAvoy wasn't there, he was going to the top of Brendan's suspect list. "Let me talk to your husband."

"What for?"

"Just put him on the phone or the sheriff is going to show up at your door."

"Fine. Here, he wants to talk to you, Steve."

"McAvoy here." The state senator made no attempt to mask his impatience.

Brendan had reached the porch and he sagged onto a chair. McAvoy hadn't taken her. Not when he was hours away. "I just wanted to make sure you were there."

"You thought I had something to do with Lauren's disappearance?" He snorted. "Like I'd dirty my hands with something like that. The press would have a field day. Here, talk to Tonia. I'm done."

There was a long pause and some whispers on the other end of the phone before Tonia came back on. "Look, we don't know anything about her disappearance. I hope you find her, but I'm going to hang up now."

He struggled to hold on to the rage that threatened to erupt. This woman was stalling when Lauren's life was on the line. "You hang up and there will be a SWAT team on its way to your place. You know more than you're saying, lady. I already know you were in hock up to your eyebrows. Where'd you get the money to pay off the sharks circling? I suspect someone paid you to hire those goons to inject the horse with some performance-impairing drugs. Windsor interfered, didn't he? I'm sure you didn't intend his death. But you're still responsible. And if you don't tell me who is behind this, you'll be responsible for your own cousin's death. These tentacles all go back to one man. I want his name." There would be time enough later to make her name the men she'd hired.

"I-I don't know what you're talking about." Her voice was muffled, and she sounded near tears.

"I think you do. Now who is he?" He doubted she'd tell him. Not with her husband right there. "If you don't want to tell me with McAvoy there, walk out of earshot. But you *will* tell me what you know."

She said nothing for a long minute. He heard shuffling and movement as well as hushed voices. He'd begun to think she wasn't going to answer when she finally cleared her throat. "Steve says I shouldn't answer you, but I don't know . . ."

"You have to tell me what you know before it's too late."

She sighed. "I never wanted anyone to get hurt. It was just a way to pay off my debts. So what if one horse that might have won didn't place? It wasn't a life or death matter."

"It ended up being just that, didn't it? And now Lauren's life is in danger."

"But it wasn't my fault! I was just paid to get him inside the barn. What he did after that had nothing to do with me."

"Who paid you, Tonia? Give me his name."

She exhaled. "It was Gary Foreshaw."

"I know him," Brendan said grimly. "Any idea where he might take her?"

She cleared her throat. "He hunts near an old defunct silver mine on government land. I've heard him joke about it being the perfect place to hide a body."

His gut clenched. "Tell me where it is." He jotted down her directions, then ended the call.

TEN

I CAN'T BREATHE.

Lauren became aware of rough carpet under her cheek and the stench of engine exhaust. Her head thumped in time with the wheels rolling over ruts. She blinked and choked back a cough. The drugged rag had fallen off her face somewhere along the way, and she pushed it farther from her nose until she couldn't smell it so strongly.

Where was she and what did he intend to do with her? The road didn't seem to be paved because the truck kept bottoming out even though it wasn't rolling very fast. She felt around for her cell phone, then remembered he'd taken it from her and tossed it away.

Her head thumped in time with the bumps, and nausea roiled in her stomach. *Breathe in and out. In and out.* Whatever he planned, it wouldn't be good. He had no choice but to kill her, and since he'd murdered the Jacobsens, he'd have no compunction about disposing of her.

The truck rolled to a stop. She forced herself to breathe

deeply, in spite of the dust, in hopes that he wouldn't be on his guard when he opened the door. Her pulse pounded in her ears. The cooling engine ticked and he still hadn't opened the door. What was he waiting for?

"I know you're awake, Lauren. I'm going to open your door, and you're going to get out without giving me any trouble or I'll just shoot you."

"Okay." Her gut clenched at the steely determination in his voice. She raised her head and got on all fours, then slid onto the backseat on the passenger side. She tried the door but it was locked. She'd only have one shot at this.

He opened his door and got out. She waited until he slammed his door, hit the key fob to unlock all the doors, then lunged forward and hit the lock button on the backseat door on the driver's side. While he fumbled for his key fob to open it again, she opened the door on the other side and threw herself out of the truck. Her feet hit the rocky dirt, but she didn't wait to get her bearings before racing away from the truck.

He shouted after her, then something zinged off a rock by her feet. He was shooting at her. She put on another burst of speed, but her left foot hit a rock and she went sprawling. A bolt of pain shot up her arm.

Before she could regain her feet, he grabbed her arm and yanked it behind her back. She struggled to get away as he tied her roughly with rope he pulled from his belt loop.

He hauled her to her feet and marched her toward a rocky hillside. "You've caused me a lot of trouble, Lauren."

"What are you going to do with me?"

"Me? I'm not going to do much of anything. It's just a shame you wandered off and got lost, then died out here. Course it happens out here in Texas."

She didn't point out the obvious fallacy of his plan. An autopsy would show chafe marks on her wrists. But as long as he left her alive, there was hope. She stumbled along with her hands tied behind her back as he dragged her near the rocks. He shoved her to the ground beside a metal stake attached to a chain and a metal ankle cuff.

She stared at the chain and realized what he planned. Her pulse throbbed in her throat, and she scrambled to her feet, then turned to run. He grabbed her and shoved her back down, then snapped the ankle cuff around her right ankle.

She lay on the hard ground and stared up at him. "Don't do this, Gary. Just let me go."

"I'm not going to prison."

She struggled to her feet. "Please, Gary. I can see you're not a violent man. You're a hero—you took in your wife's family. You're good people. Just let me go. Do the right thing."

"The right thing? That would be disastrous for me and my wife. For my family. Think of Carly. Don't you think it's better she never knows what really happened to her parents? No, you have to die. But not by my hands." He started down the hillside, his boots sliding a bit as he walked away.

She shouted after him, then gave up. If he killed Katrina's cousin, he wouldn't think twice about killing her. And he didn't even have to get his hands bloody. Once the truck pulled away, she tugged on the metal chain and tried to yank the stake out of the ground, but it was awkward to pull with her hands behind her back. She sat on the ground and tried with her legs, but when the metal cuff bit into her skin, she stopped to regroup.

There had to be a way to get loose. It was unlikely her abduction would be noticed before morning. And even when Brendan realized she was gone, he'd have no idea where to look. Even though she'd mentioned her suspicions about Gary and the fire before she went to the barn, he wouldn't have any reason to put the two things together. The fire didn't seem connected to the attacks on her.

She would have to figure this out on her own.

Something rustled off to her right, and a mournful wail lifted into the night sky. Two eyes glowed in the darkness. They were joined by more. A coyote pack. Under ordinary circumstances they tended to be cowards, but she was chained with no weapons. No defense. She couldn't even throw rocks.

⁓ℐℓℯ⁓

Rick peered out the window. "I think this is the lane."

Brendan turned his truck left at the crossroad, careful not to throw the horse trailer behind him too much. The road quickly changed to dirt. He stopped the vehicle and got out. Leaving his door open for the light, he knelt and examined the tracks. "Looks like a truck was through here recently." The fact encouraged him. Maybe they'd find her. Maybe she would still be alive.

He'd prayed hard all the way out here. Rick and Allie were praying as well. Surely God wouldn't let him find the one woman he could love only to let her die. But that was naive. He'd seen plenty of worthy men die in the line of duty. Life had a way of turning you on your head. He sent up another prayer, shook away the fear, and got back into the truck.

"I think it's only about five miles in now," Rick said.

Brendan nodded and gunned it. The truck bounced hard over the ruts left by flash floods and blistering heat, but he didn't care if he destroyed his pickup. Getting to Lauren was all he cared about. Hopefully, Angel was enduring the ride all right too.

Rick rolled his window down and leaned his head out. "I hear coyotes making a ruckus. That way." He pointed to the left.

Brendan's hands tightened on the wheel. The coyote pack could be fighting over carrion. The grisly thought left his mouth dry and his heart pounding out of his chest. That didn't mean it was Lauren's body they were fighting over. But it could.

Rick looked over at him. "I know what you're thinking. It's not her."

Brendan gave a curt nod, then reached into the console beside him and pulled out his handgun. "You need a piece?"

Rick shook his head. "I'm carrying."

Neither man spoke as the truck ate up the last miles to the mine. The coyotes were yipping and snarling as Brendan stopped by a battered sign. The name of the mine had long worn off, but the *M* and *E* were still recognizable. He threw the gearshift into Park, then leaving the engine on and the headlamps glaring, leaped out of the truck.

It was a good two miles from here and impassable except by horse. And Angel would want to find her as much as he did. He got Angel and Rick's horse out of the trailer. They were already saddled up and ready to go.

Angel snorted and tossed his head as if he sensed Lauren was in danger. Brendan ran his hand along the horse's neck. "Easy, boy." He put his foot in the stirrup and mounted.

Rick quickly mounted his horse. "This way."

The horses' hooves ate up the rough and rocky distance to the mine. Angel went from a canter to a gallop as if he sensed the urgency. He snorted as the sound of the coyotes grew louder, but he never faltered in his forward lope.

Brendan pointed at the battered wooden opening to the mine. "There it is!"

The coyotes scattered at their arrival. He dismounted and scanned the area. He cupped his hands around his mouth. "Lauren!" He carried his gun up, just in case.

Was that a shout or the wind? He took off toward the mine, his boots slipping a bit on the rocks. "Lauren!" This time he was sure he heard a cry, and he put on another burst of speed to climb the path to the mine.

A snort came from behind him, and he barely got out of the way before Angel galloped past him, headed in the direction of the cry.

Rick loped to his side. "I'm sure that's Lauren." He pulled out his revolver.

Brendan rushed up the slope after Angel and around a large rock. He stopped when he saw Lauren perched as high on a rock as she could get with the chain attached to her ankle. Angel kicked at a coyote nipping at Lauren's shoes, and the animal yelped and lurched off, then wheeled around for another go at her. Brendan shouted and fired his pistol in the air. The coyote turned and yipped, then ran off into the dark.

Angel snorted and rocked his head as if to say he'd sent the coyotes packing. He sidled closer to Lauren's perch.

Brendan raced to the rock and stuffed his gun into his belt, then held up his hands. "Let me get you down from there."

She scooted closer to the edge and dropped into his arms. He pulled her close and inhaled the sweet scent of her hair. "I thought I'd lost you." Reaching behind her, he untied the ropes from her wrists.

As soon as she was free, her arms came around, and she clung to him with ferocity, even when he tried to pull her away to look into her face. "It was Gary Foreshaw. He killed the Jacobsens. He saw my expression change at the Christmas party and knew I'd remembered."

He pressed a kiss against her hair. "I know. Tonia told me he hunted near this mine. If not for her, I wouldn't have had any idea where to find you." He finally managed to pull her away long enough to stare into her face. "You're not hurt?"

She shook her head. "Though those coyotes would have

gotten me any second if you hadn't arrived. I'd barely managed to beat them back by kicking them, but they were getting bolder."

He still couldn't believe he had her safe and sound. "I need to get this cuff off you."

Rick jogged toward them with an ax in his hand. "Found this in the bed of your truck. Hold on." He lifted it over his head and brought the blade down on the chain, which snapped instantly. "We'll have to pick the lock when we get you back to Bluebird."

Lauren leaned down to rub her ankle under the cuff. "I'm just so thankful you got here. I kept praying and praying, and God gave me a calm spirit to deal with the coyotes. I didn't panic at all. I knew you'd find me." She turned to look at her horse. "And Angel brought you right to me." She reached toward the horse, and he shuffled closer and nuzzled her hand.

Brendan pulled her close again. "Let's get you home."

EPILOGUE

CHRISTMAS MUSIC PLAYED OUTSIDE THROUGH SPEAKERS RICK had rigged. Christmas Day. Lauren sat in the swing with her head on Brendan's shoulder and the puppy in her lap. It had snowed overnight, a light, miraculous dusting that would be gone by noon. The crisp air added to her sense of contentment.

"I have news," he whispered into her hair.

She sat up though she didn't want to. "Gary Foreshaw's been captured?"

He nodded. "How did you know?"

She elbowed him. "The satisfaction in your voice."

He grinned. "I so love to see the bad guy brought to justice. Especially in this case. They caught him just across the border into Mexico. He's being extradited back to the U.S."

Her smile faded. "Tonia called me and begged me to help get her out of jail. There's nothing I can do though."

His brown eyes clouded. "She made her choices. And I'll let the authorities know she helped me find you in time. Maybe that will count for something. And if she gives the names of her hired thugs, that will go a long way too."

"I hope so." She looked off into the distant purple mountain peaks, then leaned against the back of the swing again.

They swung gently for a few moments in silence. The rest of the household would be up soon, but these next few minutes were theirs alone. Lauren wanted to hold on to them as long as she could. As far as she knew, Brendan would be going back to his dangerous job in a few more days. She knew she loved him, and he loved her, but the future was unclear. What if he forgot all about her once he was back to work and flying all over the world? What kind of relationship could they build then?

The calm she'd sought suddenly seemed elusive again. But no, she wouldn't let doubt fill her. God had led them this far. She could rest in his care. And she knew Brendan well enough to know he wasn't the kind of man to proclaim his love and then turn around and desert her.

He shifted. "Come here a minute." He pulled her onto his lap and tipped her chin up.

She met his kiss with one filled with every bit of love in her soul. His fingers tangled in her hair, and he deepened the kiss until she lost herself in a sense of wonder and rightness. This was where she belonged. They could make it work.

He broke the kiss, then cupped her face in his hands. "I have one more piece of news," he whispered.

The expression on his face made her pulse skip. "What kind of news?"

"News I think you'll like. I've accepted a medical discharge."

She gasped and searched his expression. "What does that mean?" She was afraid to hope. He'd have to tell her.

"I'm staying here. Rick needs a partner, and I'm buying into Bluebird Ranch. We're going to expand it, minister to even more kids. And you and I . . ." His lips found hers until he pulled away again. "Well, we can explore our relationship. I already know I love you, Lauren. We'll take our time, but I want to spend my life with you. Let's make sure this is right. But I want you to know where I stand."

Her pulse fluttered and she blinked, almost afraid to believe him. Could it really be true? She wrapped her arms around his neck. "I love you too, Brendan. You're a decisive man. I think I like that about you." All she wanted to do was kiss him again— for his declaration of love and for the space he was giving her.

He rubbed his thumb over her lip. "There's one more bit of news."

Her throat was so tight, she didn't know if she could speak, but she forced the words out. "I don't know if my heart can take any more."

"It's about Carly. I've applied to be her foster parent. I think I can be a good dad to her, and I know you love her already too."

"Oh Brendan! Now you've gone and made me fall in love with you all over again!" She threw her arms around his neck and kissed him. The puppy yipped in her lap as if to remind her that she'd forgotten him.

He smiled. "We'll wait to tell her once we know what we're doing. But make no mistake, Lauren. I mean to court you properly and marry you. Speak now if you want to opt out."

She leaned in close and slipped her fingers into his hair. "That sounds good to me." Her fingers wrapped in the puppy's soft fur. "I think we're going to have a houseful of kids and dogs."

When he lowered his lips to hers, she knew she'd finally found her safe place, her sanctuary. In the most unexpected place.

DISCUSSION QUESTIONS

1. Lauren warned her cousin about Steve. Do you believe a womanizer ever changes?
2. Do you believe in love at first sight? Why or why not?
3. Have you ever been betrayed by a family member? How was it different from other betrayal?
4. Have you ever had an injury that forced you to re-evaluate your life?
5. What do you do to make Christmas a calm, special time?

ALL IS BRIGHT

ONE

DELILAH CARTER'S BREATH PLUMED IN THE FROSTY AIR AS she cranked up the heater and turned her gray Toyota away from Tidewater Inn. The sun setting over the back of the inn would make a pretty postcard. Delilah had worked here for ten years, and she loved it as if she owned it. It was the only real home she'd had as an adult, and she never wanted to live anywhere else than her little suite on the third floor.

As she drove toward Hope Beach, she lowered the window and waved at Amy and Curtis Ireland putting their surfing equipment in the back of their truck. They waved back as she passed. Only those two would be crazy enough to brave December water temperatures. Even the Outer Banks was chilly this time of year. The temperature was forty-five and was expected to fall to thirty-six tonight.

Curtis's aunt must be watching the kids. Amy was the local midwife, and she'd married one of the local Coast Guard men. They were raising Curtis's niece, and they'd adopted a little girl six months ago.

Delilah's phone rang through the navigation system on the dash, and she hit the button to answer the call from Elin Summerall. "You just can't stand it, can you? I'm on my way to town to get the decorations. Everything is under control. The bride is not supposed to be stressed before the wedding. Relax."

"Easy for you to say." Elin's voice held an edge of strain. "The dress doesn't fit and will have to be taken in. The wedding is only a week away, and there is so much to do! Why on earth did I ever think a Christmas wedding was a good idea?"

"Have you been dieting?" Delilah adopted a stern tone. "With your heart transplant, you have to make sure you're eating well."

"I'm eating way too much! With so many showers and Christmas parties, I've gained five pounds. The bridal shop must have misgauged the sizing. I'll have to find a seamstress."

Delilah grinned at her friend's wheedling tone. "You know perfectly well I used to work for a bridal shop in Richmond way back when. I'll do it for you."

"You're a doll, Delilah. Is there anything you can't do? You run the inn with your hands tied behind your back, soothe guests, cook like Julia Child, and keep us all in line."

"Flattery will get you everywhere. Go get a massage or something and calm down. Talk to you later." She ended the call.

Night had quickly fallen even though it was only six. A guest at the inn with car trouble had delayed her, but her friend who ran the craft store had agreed to meet her after hours. Delilah spared a glance at the lovely ocean, ten feet below the road.

She glanced in the rearview mirror. A black truck was bearing down on her. With no lights, it was coming fast, and she veered a bit to the side of the road to let it pass.

She gripped the steering wheel and kept glancing in the rearview mirror. The truck's visor was down, obscuring the person's face in the dim twilight. It was a man though, and he sat so tall in the seat that she could see just a bit of a scruffy jaw.

She tapped her brakes just a bit to warn him to slow down, but he edged even closer. She was afraid he would ram her. What on earth? A big curve lay just ahead, and she would have to somehow make the turn without ending up in the ocean's pounding waves. Her throat closed as she saw the curve grow nearer. Easing off the gas pedal, she tapped her brakes again.

Before she could register the increase in its speed, the truck's huge chrome bumper struck her from behind. Her car fishtailed as it entered the curve, then the tires tried and failed to find purchase in the shoulder's soft gravel.

The view of the ocean grew larger in her windshield, and she fought with the wheel to steady the car. It quit careening and began to straighten, but before she could breathe a sigh of relief, another impact rattled her teeth and pushed her car to the edge.

It's going over the side.

She grabbed the handle and gave it a yank, then pushed the door open enough so she could roll out—too late. Her car left the pavement and she caught a glimpse of movement as it sailed over the edge of the hillside and down the steep slope toward the sea.

She abandoned the idea of trying to get out and steered the car as best as she could to keep it from rolling over. The car plunged into the ocean and a great plume of water washed over her windshield. The water immediately poured in her partially open door, and she held her breath as panic froze her in place.

Just like last time. If she didn't get out, she would drown just like her parents.

Terror bubbled in her chest, and her fists battered at the window. The water was deep here and so cold that it numbed her limbs. A scream formed in her throat, and she realized she was struggling to get out with her seat belt still fastened. She released it and reached for the handle. She pushed hard to try to open the door far enough to get out, but the force of the water gushing inside held it in place.

She reached for the window control and ran the window down. Water pounded her face, and she took a last deep breath before submerging so she could escape through the window.

As the vehicle dived for the bottom, the strong ocean current tugged at her coat, and she unzipped it so she could swim better. It was so dark she couldn't tell which direction led to the surface.

Then her feet touched sand, and she pushed off and swam for the surface. Spots danced in her eyes, and she wanted so badly to draw in air. Her vision was nearly gone by the time her head broke the surface and she managed to pull in oxygen.

She dog-paddled a moment until welcome air cleared her head. Lights from passing cars and a few houses oriented her to the shoreline, but she was too exhausted to do anything but bob in the waves. By the time she could summon enough determination to swim, the riptide had carried her past her car and farther out to sea.

Her muscles ached from the frigid water and the tension. Kicking off her shoes, she struck out for shore, but her tired body didn't want to cooperate. The cold numbed her mind, too, and she found it hard to focus.

No! She wouldn't give up. She'd beaten death once, and she could do it again.

She gritted her teeth and started to swim, but a big wave grabbed her and shoved her under again. Then a hard hand yanked on her arm. The dark figure pulled her toward the top, and her head broke the surface.

She blinked water out of her eyes and saw Amy swimming toward her too. Curtis had hold of one arm, and Amy took the other as they headed for the shore without speaking. Delilah couldn't have told them what happened if her life depended on it. Moments later, she lay gasping and shuddering on the shore.

Someone had tried to kill her.

⁓

Sheriff Tom Bourne sat at a table by himself in the corner of the café on Oyster Street. The spot was a local hangout smack-dab in the middle of Hope Beach's downtown. Christmas music played in the background, and the small, homey restaurant had been decked out with strings of pine garlands and tiny lights. The festive mood did little to raise his spirits. He'd be spending Christmas alone again this year unless he accepted the usual invitation to Tidewater Inn by his cousin. Some years he went and some years he didn't.

It was depressing to think that he was thirty-seven years old and might never have a family. His job kept him hopping, and his one attempt at marriage had ended after only one year when his wife, Holly, died of meningitis. While he'd loved her, their marriage had been no grand passion that had kept him single after her death. It was more a case of simple busyness.

Across the street, a spotlight illuminated a manger scene in front of city hall, and carolers gathered on the lawn. The faint refrains from "Silent Night" mingled with the canned music in the café.

The door opened and the wind ushered in Vanessa Mitchell. Her father had owned Tidewater Inn, the spectacular bed-and-breakfast outside town. He'd left it to his daughter from a previous marriage, Libby Bourne, who was married to Tom's cousin Alec. It had caused quite the sensation around town, but the siblings had all seemed to finally work things out.

Since she was alone, he waved to her. "Want to join me?"

"I thought you might be here when you weren't at your office." She slid into the chair opposite him and shrugged off her coat.

A striking beauty with brown hair tipped in purple, Vanessa had grown up quite a bit over the past few years. She was in her midtwenties and had lost the petulant expression that used to drive him crazy. She ordered coffee and soup.

He regarded her over the rim of his coffee cup. "You were looking for me?"

She nodded and tucked a strand of hair behind her ear. "I thought about calling, but I was afraid Delilah would hear me. She'd have heart failure if she knew I was making a fuss."

Delilah ran Tidewater Inn and was a treasure. Tom had thought about asking her out a few times, but she was way out of his league. Long dark curls and beautiful skin caught the attention of every man in a room. For the life of him, Tom couldn't figure out why she wasn't married.

He leaned back in his chair. "So what's up?"

"She nearly drowned tonight."

His gut clenched at the thought of Delilah at the bottom of the sea. He straightened and struggled to keep his expression from betraying him. "Is she all right?"

Vanessa's mouth was a grim line. "She would be dead if Amy and Curtis Ireland hadn't been heading home from surfing. Delilah had waved at them as she passed, and they were a few miles behind her. They saw the car lights in the water and went in after her. She was under the water and nearly gone when Curtis grabbed her."

Tom winced at the mental picture. "What happened?"

"A truck hit her and forced her off the road."

He frowned. "Deliberately?"

"She's trying to downplay it now and make out like it was an accident, but I can see the fear in her eyes. She thinks the guy ran her off the road on purpose. I think you should take a look at the accident scene."

"I should have been called to look anyway."

"One of your deputies stopped right afterward and filled out a police report. But I'd feel better if you checked it out. Something about it really gives me the creeps."

It did more than give him the creeps. "I'll check it out right now. I'll string up lights and look around before any evidence gets contaminated. Delilah isn't one to overreact. If she thinks the guy intended to hurt her, that's what happened."

"I agree, but you know how she is. She never likes to worry anyone or cause trouble. She's working on Elin and Marc's wedding stuff and didn't want to waste time on anything personal." Vanessa waited a moment as the server brought their dinner. Once they were alone again, she spread her napkin on her lap. "She's had some strange hang-ups too. Delilah has laughed it off as kids playing a prank, but I think this puts everything in a whole new light."

"How many calls?"

"About six, I think. They started two weeks ago. If anyone but Delilah answers, the caller hangs up right away. If she answers, he stays on the line and just breathes. Sometimes she hears a song playing in the background. It's always the same one too: 'Hey Pretty Girl' by Kip Moore."

He knew the song, and the lyrics in this case seemed creepy. He took a big bite of his burger, chewed, then swallowed it down with a swig of coffee before standing. "I'm going out there now."

Two

The warmth of the fire in the living room finally drove away the last of the cold lingering in Delilah's bones. This room had been recently redecorated, and the blue and white color scheme played up the high ceilings and grand fireplace of the lovely Georgian mansion they called Tidewater Inn. A gigantic Christmas tree adorned with blue and gold ornaments took up one corner of the room and caused most guests to ooh and aah.

She ran her fingers through her damp curls and smiled up at her boss and friend, Libby Bourne, who hovered anxiously. "I'm fine, Libby. Really. I think I'll go to bed early." She lifted the fabric in her lap. "As soon as I finish Josie's costume for the Christmas play at church. She's going to be a shepherd." Josie was Elin Summerall's five-year-old daughter, and Delilah adored her.

Libby's sun-streaked light-brown hair framed a striking face with bold brows and large brown eyes. Motherhood had only enhanced her beauty. In her early thirties, she was as sweet inside as she was beautiful outside. Delilah adored her, too, and their quiet talks at night after little Noah was asleep and Alec was taking care of Coast Guard paperwork.

Libby picked up Delilah's empty teacup. "I wish you'd let me call the sheriff."

The last thing Delilah wanted was to look into Tom's dark eyes and stammer out how she'd been stupid enough to almost get herself killed. She should have just pulled off the side of the road and called 911. Everything had happened so fast though. "Tom has more important things to deal with than a hysterical female."

Libby's slight frown turned to a scowl. "You're downplaying this way too much, Delilah. What about those calls too? It might all be related."

The thought was too terrifying to contemplate. "Those calls are just kids trying to scare me."

"They're doing a good job of terrifying me! I well remember searching for Nicole for weeks. I shudder at the thought of something like that happening to you." Headlights flashed through the tall windows at the front of the grand living room. "Someone's here." Libby set the cup down on a table in the entry and opened the door. "Looks like the sheriff's truck."

Delilah glanced down at her ratty green pajamas and bare feet. Her cheeks went hot at the thought of seeing Tom looking like this. There was no time to run and change or put on makeup. She grabbed a throw from the back of the sofa and wrapped it around herself like a kimono as the sheriff's heavy steps came across the porch. She watched through the door into the entry and prayed he wouldn't come in.

Libby held open the door. "Come on in, Tom. You're out and about late."

He stepped into the entry, and Delilah's pulse leaped like it always did at the sight of him. *Stupid, stupid.* Even if he was interested—which he wasn't—she liked her life right now and didn't intend to ever let a man hurt her again.

He took off his hat. "Evening, Libby. Sorry to disturb you so late, but I heard about Delilah's accident. Is she still up?"

"She's in the living room."

Tom turned and his gaze met Delilah's. Good grief, did the man have any idea what he did to her insides? Droplets of rain gleamed in his dark hair, just starting to gray at the temples, and his strong jaw and broad shoulders made her want to run into his arms for protection. Which was probably why he'd been sheriff for ten years. He inspired trust from most of the Hope Island residents. She'd found sanctuary here about the same time he became sheriff.

Libby took his coat and hung it on the coat stand by the door, then disappeared in the direction of the kitchen.

Tom stepped into the living room and examined Delilah. "You're looking mighty pretty for nearly drowning tonight."

Her laugh sounded high and forced in her ears. "Only you would say something like that to a woman in bare feet with no makeup."

He grinned, and his white teeth flashed in his tanned face before his expression turned sober. "Tell me what happened, Delilah."

She narrowed her eyes at him. "How'd you hear about it?"

"One of my deputies was investigating. When I got there, the wrecker had just managed to pull your car onto the sand."

"I'm surprised they were even able to pull it in."

"Curtis went out in his wetsuit and scuba gear to attach the hook to it. The damage to the car is pretty extensive from where the truck hit you. It's going to be a total loss."

She winced. "Vanessa told you, didn't she? She went tearing out of here shortly after I got back."

He grinned again. "Okay, yes. She found me at the café, but I would have checked it out anyway as soon as my deputy reported in. Seeing as it was you and all."

The gentleness in his tone took her aback, and she didn't quite know what to say to that. "I suppose you want to hear what happened. Have a seat." She pulled her bare feet onto the sofa with her and under the throw.

He settled beside her and took out a notebook. "When did you first notice the truck behind you?"

She launched into the event, but the retelling made her shiver again as she recalled how the truck had hit her more than once. Her description of the truck and the man wasn't going to help him much. "The truck looked like any other black truck on the road. I'm not up on models. It was older and muddy like he'd had it out on the sand or in a field."

"Any idea of his age at all?"

She shook her head. "The visor was down, so I couldn't see his face, just his jaw. Plus it went dark quickly."

"I can check with Denny's to see if anyone brought a truck in for repairs. Hitting you had to have left some damage on his truck too."

The phone jangled and she tensed. Caller ID read *Unknown* and she looked at Tom. "I've been getting calls too."

"I know. Answer it." He scooted closer.

The spicy scent of his cologne gave her the courage to grab the phone from its cradle and punch the On button. "Tidewater Inn."

The instant the call connected, she could hear the "Hey Pretty Girl" tune playing in the background. She punched on the speakerphone function so Tom could listen as well.

"Did you run me off the road today?" Her voice wobbled just a bit, and Tom touched her hand. "What do you want?"

"You know." The voice had some kind of electronic garble to it. "And you're going to pay."

The music stopped, and she realized the guy had hung up. Her hand trembled as she replaced the phone on its cradle. "I have no idea what he means."

A muscle twitched in Tom's jaw. "We're going to have to talk about your past."

Her throat closed at the thought of opening up to anyone, especially Tom. "I think I'll go to bed right now. This has been exhausting." She leaped to her feet and raced for the stairs.

Delilah kept a smile on her face as she checked out departing guests and welcomed new ones, but her sore muscles kept reminding her of that frightening brush with death. Libby had wanted her to have the doctor check her, but Delilah assured her she was fine. Saturdays were too busy to spend the morning at the doctor's office.

At three o'clock Elin arrived, wedding dress in hand. With her aqua eyes and long dark-red hair, she was going to be a beautiful bride. She smiled and held up the plastic-encased dress. "You sure you want to do this today? When the stalker was after me, I could barely function. Just thinking about what you went through last night makes me shudder."

One of the "benefits" of living on Hope Island was everyone's business made it to the coconut telegraph. Delilah didn't mind though. The good folks of Hope Island cared about each other, and she'd never had that before landing here. Before her parents died, they'd lived in a big city and life was fast paced.

She smiled and held out her hand for the dress. "I'm fine, Elin, really. I can't wait to see this on you. Let's use the butler's pantry. I've got some pins in there, and I can lock the door." The weight of the dress in her hands told her it was likely encrusted with beads and sequins. That could be challenging to take in, but Elin deserved any effort.

She led her friend to the butler's pantry off the dining room. The large room held floor-to-ceiling cabinets stuffed with various serving pieces and cooking items that weren't used as frequently. This was "her" spot though, the place where she planned the meals and immersed herself in food. Something about feeding people made her feel complete. She'd learned to make most of the dishes she still cooked today in her mother's kitchen. Today the aroma of her seafood curry wafted from the kitchen.

She'd loaded one drawer with emergency sewing supplies like pins and sticky tape, and her Pfaff sewing machine occupied a discreet corner to zip up torn tablecloth edging or napkins.

She hung the dress on a hook attached to the side of a cabinet and unzipped it. The sun shining through the large mullioned windows gleamed on the beads and sequins, and she caught her breath. "Oh, Elin, it's gorgeous." Pearls encrusted the fitted bodice of the mermaid dress, and more pearls and sequins glittered down the skirt. "Let's try this on you."

Elin was already shucking her jeans and sweatshirt. Delilah slipped it over her friend's head, then zipped and buttoned up the back. "Turn around, all the way around, and let me see." She eyed the fit as Elin spun slowly around. "The bodice fits nicely, but the waist and hips need taken in a bit. It's going to take a few days because of all the beads and sequins, but we have time, and it will be gorgeous."

Elin's worried frown eased. "Delilah, you are the best ever! Thank you so much. You're already doing so much. Is there anything I can do to help?"

Delilah shook her head. "It's under control. I've already made the mints and frozen them, and I've purchased all the decorations. The tent is reserved and so are the tables. I just have to do the flower arrangements and make the cake."

"'Just.' You make it sound so easy, when it's a boatload of work. I'm terrible at flowers and baking, so I won't be much help there."

"Your job is to relax and not turn into a bridezilla." Delilah unfastened the buttons and unzipped the dress, releasing Elin from it. She eased the heavy weight over Elin's head and hung the dress back on its hanger. "How is Marc holding up?"

"Like a trooper. He's ready to get it done."

"You can't blame him. He was ready to get married a month after he proposed."

"And we'd planned to do that, but his mother had a fit and wanted us to have a proper wedding. I didn't want to start my marriage on the outs with the in-laws, so I talked him into doing what she wanted. I think it was the right thing to do, but I'll be so glad when the hullabaloo is over. This would have been so easy if we'd just eloped to St. Croix like we wanted."

Delilah's chest compressed when she thought about how certain Elin was of Marc's love. How wonderful it must be to know Marc would never abandon her. It was something Delilah likely would never experience. At thirty-three, the men weren't exactly breaking down her door. It would be a dream come true to have a real family and a loving husband who was always a constant companion.

Delilah zipped the dress back up. Standing at the window, she saw a familiar truck coming toward the inn. "It's the sheriff."

Elin joined her. "He probably has more questions about

what happened yesterday. I'll get out of here and let you talk to him. I asked Marc to look into it with his FBI resources as well, and he said he would if Tom needs anything from him."

Delilah followed her to the entry where Elin put on her coat. The doorbell rang as Delilah reached for the knob, and her pulse kicked when she looked up into the sheriff's kind brown eyes. "Hi, Tom."

His gaze went to Elin and back again. "Hope I'm not disturbing you."

"Not at all. Elin is just leaving. Come on in."

Elin greeted him, then headed for her car while he brought the scent of the sea and cool air into the foyer with him. Delilah closed the door. He would want to take up where they left off last night. Where could she take him to talk? Guests were in the living room, and the staff was continuing to prepare dinner so the kitchen was out.

"You mind walking along the beach? I know it's a little nippy today, but we have a full house inside."

He shrugged. "Born and raised on this island. A little December wind won't put my nose out of joint."

She pulled on her coat and tugged a knit cap down over her ears before stepping out to the porch. The expansive space looked out on the coastline, and she never tired of watching the sea. What was she even going to say to Tom? She'd worked hard to keep her secrets out of island talk, but she couldn't hide any longer.

She said nothing as she led the way out toward the water. Gulls swooped and squawked overhead, and the outgoing tide had deposited kelp and shells on the sand. The cool breeze tugged at her hat.

She stooped and picked up a rock, then flung it into the whitecaps. "I suppose you want to know why I ran off like that last night."

"It'd be a good start. I won't judge you for anything, Delilah. Nothing you could say would shock me. This is something from your past, isn't it?"

A boulder formed in her throat, and she nodded. "I'd hoped it wasn't, but I think so." She pinched the bridge of her nose. "I was so young and stupid. My parents died when I was ten, and I was in one Maine foster home after another. I met Pete when I was eighteen, and all I really wanted to do was to get out from under the worst of the homes I'd been in. I knew Pete had a drug problem, but I thought I could help him."

Her laugh was harsh and forced in her ears. "Stupid, I know. I was with him for five years before he got picked up for selling heroin. I testified against him, and he went to prison. I knew he or his cronies would want revenge, so I took off and landed here."

"So you think he's out of prison now and trying to kill you in retaliation?"

"I don't know what else it could be." The thought of seeing Pete again filled her with terror. He'd changed after he got hooked on heroin, and she'd felt his fist on more than one occasion.

Tom's hand came down on her forearm, and he turned her around to face him. "I'll see what I can find out about his whereabouts. Don't you worry though, Delilah. I'll keep you safe."

With Tom's stalwart form beside her, she felt safe and protected. She searched his gaze and nodded. "You're a good man, Tom."

Something sparked between them, but she spun away so she wouldn't have to identify it.

THREE

TOM'S OFFICE WAS AS FAMILIAR AS HIS FAVORITE NIKES. IT held a battered desk and a metal filing cabinet, both overflowing with stacks of paper. He knew exactly what was in every stack and how far down. The cleaning lady was told only to sweep the floor and empty the trash. After hanging up his coat on a rack by the door, he fired up his computer and typed in the name Delilah had given him.

Pete Johnson was in prison. He'd been out for a year before being picked up again, this time for attempted murder. Tom leaned back in his old chair and stared at the screen. The possibility of parole wasn't for another ten years. Could he have hired someone to come after Delilah? It didn't seem likely, but she hadn't mentioned anyone else who held a grudge.

Though he hated to do it, he typed in her name to run a check. It felt like an invasion of her privacy, but he had to know everything if he had any chance of preventing the guy from striking again. The next time he might succeed.

While the computer did its thing, he rose and made a fresh pot of coffee. The stuff in the pot had been there since yesterday morning. As he turned he saw his cousin Alec Bourne standing in the doorway. "Hey, come on in. I was just putting coffee on."

Still in his Coast Guard uniform, Alec stepped into the office and closed the door behind him. "Hope I'm not disturbing you."

"Not at all. I was just seeing what I could uncover about the attack on Delilah. That why you're here?"

Alec nodded and dropped into the chair opposite Tom's desk. He was a chief petty officer who had fallen for Libby the minute she arrived on the island. "Find out anything?"

"It's not her old boyfriend." Tom told him what he'd discovered. "Can you think of anything Delilah has said that might indicate another problem? You've been around her daily for two years now."

Alec plucked a pencil off Tom's desk and began to flip it through his fingers like a baton. His brow creased as he thought a moment. "She is pretty private. I don't know that I've ever heard her take a call from anyone other than Hope Beach residents. I don't even know where she's from originally."

"She was born in Maine." Warmth expanded in his chest as he realized he knew more about Delilah than even her closest friends. "She was in a bunch of foster homes. It was a hard life from the sound of it."

Alec raised a brow. "Careful there, cuz. I've seen the way you look at her when you think no one is watching. You ever going to get the gumption to ask her out?"

"What makes you think she'd go?" Tom shot back. "I haven't seen her returning the looks."

"Libby thinks you two would make a cute couple."

Tom shook his head and huffed out a laugh. "Spoken like a newlywed."

"Hey, I've been married two years."

"A wealth of experience for sure." Tom grinned to take the sting out of his words. "What did you make of the attack last night? Did she talk about it over breakfast?"

"She's trying to make out that maybe it was an accident, but you and I both know that's not true. The truck bumped into her repeatedly."

Tom nodded. "I checked the tracks again this morning. He intended to hurt her."

"You think it was attempted murder or maybe just to give her a good scare?"

"Some cars wouldn't have made it all the way to the water, but her car was angled just right to plunge into the surf. It's hard to know if he realized that or just wanted to frighten her half to death. Either way, I will find him."

Tom's cell phone rang, and he saw Josh Holman's name on the screen. Josh worked with Alec and Curtis. "Hey, Josh, you looking for Alec? He's right here."

"Nope, it's you I want. I think while I was out on a mission, my truck got stolen yesterday and was taken for a joyride. Kids probably. When I got back in this morning, it was parked in a different spot on the lot, and the grill is all smashed up like it hit something."

Tom straightened and grabbed a pad of paper and pen. "It's black, isn't it? A Chevy?"

"Yeah, and it's not worth that much so I can't turn it in to insurance. It doesn't even have a working airbag. I wanted you to know we've got some wild kids running around."

"I think it might be more than that." He told Josh about the truck used in the attack on Delilah.

Josh whistled. "I probably shouldn't get in it or anything until you have a chance to check it out. I'll have Sara come get me and I'll leave it unlocked. It's in the west side of the Coast Guard parking lot."

"Thanks, buddy, I'll send out a forensics tech." That would take a while to come from the state police, but at least he might get some evidence. Hair, fiber, something. He ended the call and told Alec what Josh had found.

"This guy thought of everything. He probably didn't leave any evidence," Alec said.

"That would be just our luck." His computer had finished the search so he leaned forward to look at the screen. "I ran a search on her to see if anything turned up."

Alec winced. "I hate that you had to do that, but I guess it's necessary. Anything?"

Tom whistled softly. "Her parents were drowned when their car ran into a river. She witnessed the whole thing and barely survived herself. No wonder she buried herself here and never wanted to go anywhere else." He shut down his computer and rose. "I think I'd better talk to her again."

Hopeful Coffee on Oyster Street was quiet this time of year, just like every other shop in Hope Beach. Once the weather turned cold, only locals braved the chilly ride over on the ferry from Hatteras. Delilah carried the two steaming mochas and a plate of bagels with cream cheese to a back table where her friend waited for her.

Vanessa took one of the cups from her. "Thanks. So you're not going to kill me for telling the sheriff?"

Delilah put the plate on the table and sat across the table from Vanessa. "He didn't give you up willingly." She took a sip of the chocolatey concoction, then licked the whipped cream off her lips. "How are things with Gage?"

Her friend's face lit up. "Wonderful. You were so right about Keith. It wasn't until I broke it off that I realized how controlling he really was. Gage isn't like that at all. He's kind and warm, and he wants to please me. With Keith, it was his way or the highway."

"Has Keith quit calling you?"

Vanessa tucked a short brown strand of purple-tipped hair behind one ear. "Finally. The last call was two weeks ago. I think he finally got the message. I told him if he called again,

I was going to tell Tom he was stalking me. That must have gotten through to him."

"I'm so glad you broke it off."

Vanessa's blue eyes sparkled. "My protector. You mother everyone."

Delilah made a face. "Sorry, I can't help it. I hope you never get another call from him."

"Me too. At first Keith seemed so sweet and caring. He was always calling to see how my day went. I got a little present from him about every day. Then all that attention turned suffocating when he moved close enough to see my house and notice anytime I left. It happened so gradually that I didn't see it until you pointed it out."

Vanessa took another sip of her coffee, and her eyes were coy over the top of the coffee cup. "The sheriff came right out, didn't he? I could see the concern on his face. All it would take is a little encouragement for him to ask you out."

"Why is it that every time someone is in love they want to make sure everyone else is in a relationship? I'm happy just like I am. I love my life. I wouldn't change a thing."

Liar. She wanted the same thing Vanessa did. A real family, not just a family circle she was lucky enough to be invited into.

Vanessa picked up a bagel with strawberry cream cheese. "What's up with that, Delilah? You're always so willing to jump in and help everyone, but at the same time, you keep most people at arm's length. I was lying in bed last night thinking about how I consider you my best friend, but I don't know much about your early life. You never talk about it. We talk about things going on here, but never about what it was like for you growing up."

Heat scorched Delilah's cheeks. "I'm a boring topic. Besides, it's in the past and I don't want pity."

Vanessa's brows rose and she set the bagel back down. "What happened? Some things never get better until you drag them out of the closet and let the light hit them."

The bite of bagel Delilah had just taken tasted like sand, but she swallowed it down with a sip of her mocha. She hadn't talked about all this in years, and now questions seemed to be coming at her from every side. Maybe it was a sign from God that she needed to wipe away the cobwebs and let the sunlight in to the deepest corners of her life. The thought made her lungs compress.

She took another sip of coffee to delay, then set the cup back on the black-and-white checkered tablecloth. She told Vanessa about her parents' deaths. "I was in the car, too, and should have drowned, but there was a pocket of air in the backseat from how the car landed in the water. I remember screaming and screaming until some guy opened the back door and got me out."

The color drained from Vanessa's face. "You watched your parents drown? Yesterday must have been doubly terrifying. No wonder you don't like to talk about it. I'm so sorry. Where did you go then?"

"Lots of foster homes."

Vanessa winced. "What happened to cause the accident? Did you ever hear?"

Delilah thought about it. "I remember the steering wasn't working right. Dad said something about the power steering pump going out. He knew it was acting up, but he hadn't had the money to get it fixed. He was a mechanic." Even at her age, the smell of grease brought back her dad.

"Why didn't your parents release their seat belts and get out or at least get in the back with you to the bubble of air?"

"Dad had hit his head and wasn't moving. His eyes were closed. Mom kept trying to get loose, but I think she was so panicked that she wasn't flipping the seat belt right." Her eyes burned. "I should have helped somehow. Gone into the front and gotten her free."

"You were a kid, Delilah. There was nothing you could do." Tears glimmered in Vanessa's eyes too. "Did you have siblings?"

"I had an older brother. He wasn't with us because he had just gone off to a new job in California."

"Do you ever see him?"

She shook her head. "I've never been able to find him. When our parents died, the authorities tried to contact him, but they couldn't find him. His name was Adam." She hadn't even said his name in so long, and a deep longing swept over her. How long had it been since she'd looked for him? At least ten years. It wouldn't hurt to look again.

FOUR

THE WIND BLEW OFF THE OCEAN IN GUSTS AS TOM WALKED out onto the Tidewater Pier, where a figure sat with her feet dangling off the edge. Fishing pole in hand, Delilah huddled inside her jacket with the hood up. As he approached, he saw two striped bass in the cooler beside her.

Wind-tossed dark curls peeked out the sides of her hood as she turned a smile his direction, which made him gulp as he settled beside her. "Looks like a good day. Enough for dinner?"

She pushed her hood down and nodded. "We only have two rooms rented this time of year, so I think I'll have enough. Those are big ones."

"Should be good eating." Gulls swooped overhead as they enjoyed the bit of winter sunshine. "I wanted to let you know that I checked up on Pete Johnson."

She inhaled, and her hands shook a bit as she pulled in her pole and laid it aside. "Is he here on the island?"

Her hand was cold when he put his over it. "He's in prison, Delilah. He got out for a year but went right back in for attempted murder. He's not getting out for a long, long time."

Her lashes swept down over the deep blue of her eyes, and she clung to his hand. When she looked up again, a frown crouched on her brow. "Then who ran me off the road?"

"Wish I knew. We won't find him with a check on trucks. He stole Josh Holman's truck and used it to ram you, then returned it. Josh told me about it today."

"I'd hoped we'd track him down quickly."

That had been Tom's hope too. "The caller yesterday said you knew what he wanted. Can you think of anyone else who might have a grudge against you? There has to be something."

She shook her head. "I'll think about it, but I'm not the type who goes around making enemies. I like most people, and I try to be a peacemaker in everything. It's so odd."

Her fingers entwined around his in a trusting way that made him want to scale castle walls for her. "I've asked all the bed-and-breakfasts and hotels in town to give me a list of visitors. This time of year we don't have many, so it should be easy enough to investigate."

"Someone could be visiting friends or relatives too."

"True enough. What about the two rooms you have rented? Ever seen the visitors before?"

"Oh yes, they are both regulars. They've been coming here for Christmas for years. Lovely people."

"I'll still want their names so I can check them out. E-mail me anything you know about them."

"All right, but I know it's not them." She still made no move to pull her hand away.

Several dolphins leaped in the water off to their left, and

the sound of the waves was a soothing backdrop. Tom considered asking her to dinner, but the timing didn't seem right with her on edge from the scare. Or was it his own nervousness about being turned down?

"You probably shouldn't be out here alone, you know," he said. "Someone could come right out here and toss you off the pier."

"I'm a strong swimmer."

"There's a riptide that runs the shoreline this time of year. And hypothermia can set in fast. You've got to start thinking smart about this guy. Whatever game he's playing isn't over." With reluctance he removed his hand and stood. "I'd better get to finding him. You holding up okay?"

"I'm keeping busy with the wedding approaching. Are you attending?"

"Wouldn't miss it. You're pulling it all together for Elin, aren't you? More of your mothering?"

Smiling, she rose. "You're the second person to mention that today. Am I that bad?"

"I think it's sweet the way you care for everyone." The words were out of his mouth before he could call them back. "I mean, most people think only of themselves, but you're different." Her gaze was locked to his, and he took a step nearer. "I like that. You care, and it shows." His voice went gruff, and he stuffed his hands in his pockets so he wouldn't take her in his arms.

What was wrong with him? He usually had no trouble keeping women at arm's length, but lately he'd realized how empty his life had become. He existed at the fringes of his friends' and family's orbits with no real life of his own. His work had been everything to him after Holly's death ten years ago. It had been enough for a long time, but it wasn't as satisfying anymore. Holly had been a sweet wife, and though he hadn't intended to lock himself up in a house alone for the rest of his life, that's exactly what he'd done. How did he go about breaking free of the reins that pulled him in every time he thought of dating? He hadn't thought he'd be such a coward about being hurt again. Some protector he was when he couldn't throw off his own fear.

Delilah touched his arm. "Thanks for trying to help, Tom. It means more than you know."

He touched his fingers to his hat. "Talk to you soon. Don't go out alone after dark. No walks down the road or along the beach unless Alec is with you, okay?"

"Yes, Sheriff Worrywart." The hint of a smile lifted her lips, and her eyes were soft. "I'll e-mail you with those names."

He nodded and walked back down the pier toward shore. If he turned around, would she be watching? He couldn't bring himself to check.

The last of the dying sunlight shone through the double windows in Delilah's studio apartment on the top floor of Tidewater Inn. The room was large with a queen bed taking up one side of the room, and a small love seat and two chairs occupied the other side. Her small kitchenette held a single sink, a short run of counter, and a small fridge. She'd brought her sewing machine up from the butler's pantry to work on the wedding dress.

Her back ached from sewing beads and sequins back into place. She reclined and rubbed her burning eyes. The wedding dress needed only to be pressed now, and it was ready for the wedding.

Lifting the heavy folds, she returned the dress to the padded hanger and raised it to the tall hook on the wall. Elin would be so pleased. Someone tapped at her door, and she went to open it.

Her hair in a ponytail and dressed in yoga clothes, Libby stood outside. Her face was pink and slightly damp. "I'm probably smelly from my workout, but I'm so mad I could spit."

Delilah stood aside. "What's wrong? You look hot. I've got cold-pressed green juice in the fridge. Want some?" At Libby's nod, Delilah grabbed a bottle and handed it to her hot friend. "Sit down and tell me what's wrong."

Libby dropped into one of the chairs and took a swig of the cold juice. "I got a call from the florist, and they won't be able to deliver the flowers you ordered for Elin's wedding. They're going out of business."

"You're kidding! Without at least fulfilling the orders they have?" Delilah's mind raced trying to figure out how to get the flowers in only five days. While the order wasn't huge, it was specific with Elin really wanting lily of the valley in her bouquet.

Libby took another gulp of her juice. "I haven't told Elin yet. She doesn't need any more stress."

Delilah fixed her with a stare. "Neither do you."

"I'm fine. You've already got so much on your plate. I can make some calls for you and see if I can find the flowers."

Delilah fell silent as she thought about it. While she didn't want to add to Libby's workload, finding more flowers was going to be a hassle. And she didn't know how reliable the other florists were. She'd trusted Hope Beach Floral, and they had always come through for her. "I probably ought to make a trip to Kill Devil Hills and actually look at what they've got."

"Like you have time for that." The flush on Libby's face was beginning to fade. "Though Tom has a nice big boat, and he could run you over in a jiffy. Much faster than waiting on the ferry."

Delilah wagged a finger at her. "I see your nefarious plan."

"Brilliant, isn't it?" Libby's grin was unrepentant. "I'm not going to let up until you at least go out with him. This would be an awesome first date." Her gaze wandered away, and she took another sip.

Delilah narrowed her eyes at her friend. "Spill it. What aren't you telling me?"

Color washed up Libby's face again. "I already asked him, okay? I knew you'd never let me take on some of the work, and I knew you'd want to go to some other towns. So I called him."

Delilah gaped. "Libby, you didn't!"

Libby's chuckle held a bit of unease as if she wasn't sure

Delilah wasn't going to strangle her. "He practically fell over himself in his eagerness to say yes."

The mental image of that made Delilah choke back a laugh. "You should have talked to me first. So when did he agree to take me? I need to go right away, tomorrow." She might be able to get out of it if Tom had plans for the next few days.

"He's coming at seven in the morning." Libby looked smug. "You didn't think I would let any loophole develop in my plan, did you?"

Delilah slapped her palm against her forehead. "Why is everyone trying to fix me up with Tom? I mean, he's a nice man and everything. I like him, I do. Are you trying to get rid of me or something? You want to hire someone else to take my job?" The thought of someone else in this small apartment and behind the reception desk gave her pause. "I'll just let him know it's not necessary."

"You'll do no such thing! You need a fast turnaround on those flowers, and this is the way to do it. You'll have a great time too." Libby rose and went to throw open Delilah's closet. "What are you going to wear?"

Delilah sighed and joined her at the closet door. "Jeans and a T-shirt." She reached in and grabbed the shirt she usually wore for painting, then held it up to her chest. "How about this one? Goes with my eyes, doesn't it?" She batted her lashes at Libby, who burst into laughter.

Libby snatched it away and stuck it back in the closet. "I think these khaki slacks with this blue-and-white sweater would look nice. And those cute red wedges you never wear."

"I'm picking out flowers, not trying to get Tom's attention." But she let Libby lay out the clothes on a straight-backed chair. "I can't even remember the last time I wore anything but jeans or yoga pants."

"It's high time then." A self-satisfied smile played around Libby's lips. "Tom won't know what hit him."

"You're expecting way too much out of tomorrow," Delilah warned.

"We'll see. Lunch in Kill Devil Hills would be nice. Alec has a car parked in a lot at Kitty Hawk, and you guys can use it to run around." She dug a set of keys out of her pocket and dropped them into Delilah's palm. "Have fun."

"Slave driver." Delilah walked her to the door, but she couldn't help a tiny niggle of excitement.

FIVE

DELILAH HADN'T SAID MUCH WHEN TOM ARRIVED AT Tidewater Inn and escorted her to his boat at the pier. The day was around forty-five degrees, and he put her in the warmest spot he could find right next to him in the bridge. He'd brought several blankets and wrapped her in one before they got started. Only a few clouds floated in the pale-blue sky, but the sea breeze zipped right through his Windbreaker.

The boat rose and fell with the whitecaps as he turned the boat toward Kill Devil Hills. A dolphin zipped alongside the boat for a while before zooming off to join its pod. He glanced at her from the corner of his eye. "You okay?"

The wind lifted her dark curls as she turned her head and smiled at him. "Fine. Thanks for bringing me today. How'd you get off work?"

"Even a sheriff can use a vacation day. I haven't taken any time off this year at all. I was due." Had Libby coerced her into coming? Asked him to bring Delilah before talking to her? He wouldn't ask Libby that for any amount of money though. For one thing, he didn't want to know if it was true.

What would Delilah think if she knew he was looking for her brother? When running the check on her past, he found out she hadn't heard from her brother in all these years, so he'd decided to try to find Adam for her as a surprise. But the guy hadn't popped up in his search. It was better not to mention his investigation to Delilah just in case he was dead.

Homes along the shore were decked out with driftwood "trees" decorated with ornaments that shimmered in the sunlight. They should be pretty all lit up. Maybe the excursion would take long enough that their return would be after dark.

Delilah leaned forward as he docked the boat on the sound side in Kitty Hawk. "It's pretty deserted." She pointed to a black vehicle. "There's Alec's truck."

Was that a hint of excitement in her voice? At least she was smiling. Whatever had been eating her seemed to have left with the sight of the festive decorations. He helped her off the boat, and she handed him the truck keys.

The Chevy truck started with the first try. "Where to first?"

She consulted a note on her phone. "There are quite a few florists in the area. Let's start with one in Kill Devil Hills. I could use some coffee too."

"I am reading your mind. Front Porch Café, right?" He headed the truck toward Highway 158.

"My mouth is already watering."

He thought about all the things he could say. Like how pretty she looked and how perfect her skin was in the bright morning sunshine. Or how much he liked the navy jacket against her dark curls. In the end he barely mustered up, "I like red shoes."

Her face went a little pink, and she looked down at her red wedges. "Me, too, but I don't usually have the courage to wear them. Libby talked me into it though. She said they would feel festive and Christmassy. I've been so focused on the wedding that I've barely thought about Christmas beyond what I'm fixing for dinner."

"What do you say we make a day of it and get your Christmas shopping finished then? I need to get a few things too." Did he just say that? He shot her a glance to see if she was offended, but she turned her head to smile at him, and the tension in his chest released.

"A guy who offers to take a girl shopping is one of a kind." She narrowed her eyes at him. "You trying to bribe me or something?"

"Well, I wouldn't say no to a pan of your famous chocolate-and-peanut butter brownies."

"We'll see if you deserve them. It all depends on how much you rush me in the bookstore."

The banter between them made him grin down at her. Maybe she liked him just a little. "Bookstore?"

"I like to buy books as gifts. There's the perfect book for everyone."

He crossed his arms over his chest. "And what book would be perfect for me?"

Her perfectly shaped dark brows lifted, and she looked him

over. "Hmm. You're a man's man. You'd charge hell with a water pistol, but you have a softer side you don't like to show. I didn't quite see it myself until you offered to go shopping. I mean, what man does that?" Her laughter rang out, and her eyes sparkled. "So I'll have to think about that book for you."

"Does that mean I'm invited for Christmas dinner?" He navigated the traffic as he watched for mile marker six.

"Aren't you always?" She turned away to look out the window. "There's the café. I can almost taste that Morning Glory Muffin."

His elation burst like an overfilled water balloon. Maybe her banter was because she viewed him as one of the family. He needed to be careful or he'd get hurt.

He glanced at her from the corner of his eye. Doggone it, no. Protecting himself was his usual reaction. Delilah was special and he'd always known it. He was going for broke on this, and he'd let the chips fall where they may. If she ended up trampling his heart, at least he would go down knowing he'd given it his all.

───

This was the fourth florist, and Tom was beginning to think no one would be able to help them. Once again they were told that the lilies of the valley Elin wanted were hard to find even in season, let alone at Christmastime. Several offered white baby's breath instead, but they thanked them and continued the search.

They exited the shop, and Tom blinked in the sunshine and stepped to Delilah's side so his bulk shielded her from the worst of the wind. "We're beginning to run out of florists. We could go on up to Richmond maybe."

Delilah nibbled on her lip, a trait he found endearing. "I'm beginning to think I need to tell Elin what's going on."

"You're Wonder Woman, but there's a limit to even what you can do. You can't fabricate flowers out of thin air."

"I would if I could. I so hate to disappoint Elin." She sighed and pulled out her phone. "I'm going to call her."

Tom listened to her side of the conversation and saw her shoulders relax. When she ended the call, he took her arm and steered her toward the street. "She's okay with baby's breath?"

"Yes, thank goodness. Elin is not a bridezilla in any way. She was a lot less stressed about it than I am." She stepped off the curb and into the parking lot to cross to the truck, parked on the far side of the lot.

The hair on the back of Tom's neck prickled, and he looked around at the people hurrying to and from the shops in the small strip mall. His intuition told him they were being watched, but no one appeared to be taking undue note of them. In an apartment above a card shop, a curtain twitched, and he shaded his eyes to stare at the window.

"Something wrong?" Delilah's voice held alarm.

"A goose walked over my grave, I guess." He never dialed down his situational awareness, not even during social occasions. No sense in worrying her though.

He guided her to the truck and opened her door. A white

envelope lay on the passenger seat with her name scrawled across it in bold lettering. "Hold on."

She craned her neck to look around him. "A card?"

"Looks like it. I had a feeling someone might be watching us, but I'd hoped it was my imagination. Guess not." He pulled latex gloves out of his pocket and put them on before picking up the envelope by one corner.

It wasn't sealed, so he opened the flap and pulled out the card. The handmade card cover was a picture of Tidewater Inn taken by the shore. His gut tightened, and he flipped it open to read the message inside.

I'll be here when you least expect me.

Delilah gasped. He put his arm around her waist and pulled her against him. "He's just trying to scare you."

"He's doing a good job." Her voice shook and she bit her lip. "I wish I knew who was doing this and why. I don't have a single enemy. It makes no sense."

"There are a lot of disturbed people out there. I want you to continue to go through every relationship you've ever had, every exchange in the grocery store or parking lot. Maybe something will come to mind that will help us figure this out."

"Okay." She blew out a shaky breath. "I think I need sustenance. The smell of those enchiladas is making me hungry. And I need more coffee if I'm going to face any more rejections by florists."

He grinned at the way she was able to push away her fear and soldier on. "Bad Bean Baja Grill it is! They make the best mahimahi tacos on the planet."

"And their Baja salad has jicama in it. I love it."

They walked toward the street, and he found himself taking her hand. She didn't pull away but, instead, curled her fingers around his in a companionable way as if they'd done it a million times. Once they were seated side by side in a booth inside the brightly decorated restaurant, he smoothed the card again and looked it over.

Her shoulder brushed his. "The guy made it himself out of card stock."

"Yeah." He studied the bold lettering. "Clearly a man's handwriting."

"Something about it seems familiar. When I get back to the inn, I think I'll go over the guest registry and see if anyone's signature looks like this guy's lettering."

"Good idea. And I'll hang on to this for evidence."

The server took their orders and brought their drinks, iced tea for both of them. "I thought you wanted coffee," he said when the server departed.

She wrinkled her nose. "Not restaurant coffee, coffee shop coffee. I'm picky."

"I used to be, before I worked in law enforcement. Now I'll even take day-old coffee if I have to."

She shuddered. "You're my hero."

He plucked her hand off the table. "I'd like to be." Staring into her blue eyes, he felt something shift between them. Awareness sparked in her eyes, but she didn't look away. Since she probably wasn't going to answer his statement, he felt the need to fill the silence somehow and cleared his throat.

"I'm going to court you, Delilah. That's an old-fashioned word, but I'm an old-fashioned guy. If nothing else, this situation you've found yourself in has shown me clearly I have feelings for you. Feelings I've buried for the past couple of years, but I won't do it anymore. You can tell me to go away if you want, but I'll keep knocking on your door until you give us a chance."

She caught her breath, and her fingers tightened on his. "What if one of us gets hurt?"

He put on his best Westley impression. "'Life is pain, Highness. Anyone who says differently is selling something.'"

She burst into a giggle and covered her mouth. "Mr. He-Man Sheriff has watched *The Princess Bride*? Color me shocked."

Tom shrugged. "I have a sister, and she forced it on me."

"I like a guy who listens to his sister."

She still hadn't taken her hand away from his, and he took hope from that.

SIX

"*I'M GOING TO COURT YOU.*"

As Delilah browsed through Island Books and picked out Christmas gifts for the people she cared about, she kept catching sight of Tom's dark head over the top of a bookshelf. Had he really meant it? It had taken real courage to just up and declare himself to her that way, and she didn't know what to make of it.

With her purchases bagged while he browsed the children's books to find something for Libby and Alec's son, Noah, she settled onto a love seat to wait for him.

"Delilah Carter, I never expected to see you here."

That energetic voice could only belong to Pearl Chilton, Hope Island's postmistress. She was Libby and Vanessa's aunt, and Delilah adored her, along with everyone else in town. Barely topping five feet and nearly as round as she was tall, Pearl was past retirement age, but it would take an act of God to get her out of the run-down post office. Her green eyes were inquisitive as she tugged her purse strap over her shoulder.

Delilah put her bags onto the floor to make room for Pearl. "Just doing some Christmas shopping, same as you."

Pearl sank onto the cushion beside Delilah. "Is Libby around too?"

"Nope." There was no way in the world Delilah could hide the fact she was here with Tom. He was bound to show up before Pearl left. "I-I came over with Sheriff Bourne. I had a glitch in the flowers for Elin's wedding, so he offered to run me over on his boat."

Pearl tipped her head to one side. "You're getting flowers at a bookstore?"

"Well, no. I arranged for the flowers, then we both decided to grab some Christmas presents here."

"Dinner later at The Black Pelican, no doubt."

She'd never fool those wise old eyes. "There was some mention of that, yes."

Pearl sat back with a satisfied smile. "I'm glad to see you having some fun, Delilah. You work too hard and you never take time for yourself, and Tom has been alone too long."

"His wife died, but that's about all I know."

Pearl nodded. "A sad story. She was a schoolteacher and caught meningitis, which isn't common in an adult. She was prone to migraines, and she refused to go to the doctor until the infection was pretty far gone. The Coast Guard airlifted her to Richmond, but it was too late. Poor Tom was just a deputy back then, and it hit him hard. She was pregnant, too, so it was a double blow."

Delilah sucked in a breath. "That's terrible."

"It was indeed. I've never known him to show any interest in another woman before now. I'm sure he'll tell you all about it. He's a good man."

"Yes, yes, he is." How did she go about changing the subject? This whole idea of any kind of relationship was too new for Delilah.

Pearl pushed a salt-and-pepper lock out of her eyes. "You look like you want to run."

"I don't have any business dating anyone," Delilah blurted out. "I sure can't compete with a memory like that."

"Compete? Is that how you view letting someone care about you, honey? Is that why you do so much for everyone else? You feel you have to prove yourself? People love you for who you are. You don't have to work so hard at it."

Delilah bit back the gasp that gathered in her throat. "I-I need to run to the restroom. Be right back." Her cheeks burned as she rushed away.

Thankfully, the bathroom was empty, and she locked the door behind her, then splashed cold water on her face. Pearl's observation had been like an arrow to the heart. She patted a paper towel on her dripping face and stared in the mirror.

A thirty-three-year-old woman with haunted eyes stared back at her. Any carefree spirit she'd once possessed had been knocked out of her after being shuttled around from home to home. Then Pete had come along, and she'd walked on eggshells when she was with him because he was so volatile. After failing her mother, then failing every other relationship from that of a foster kid to her romance with Pete, she'd been afraid to try to do more than be the friend in the background.

Was it time to go for more, to actually want something for herself? And was that even okay with God? Since she'd failed so miserably, she poured everything into being the best person, the best Christian she could be. Any other desire she'd called selfish and had tried to bury.

Was this an invitation from God to walk through an unknown door? A tiny sprout unfurled inside and reached for the sunshine of hope. Maybe it was, and she wasn't going to pull it up by the roots, not this time.

Delilah checked everything off her list as she looked around. The large greenhouse on the Tidewater Inn property had been transformed to a winter wonderland with fake snow, evergreen trees decked out in white lights, and wreaths in all the right places. More lights hung around the greenhouse, and it would be spectacular at dark. A red carpet runner would lead from the entrance to the other side. And the temperature had reached a balmy sixty today. By dark, another hour, it would still be fifty-five.

Her gaze cut to the flowers. There were no lilies of the valley in the sprays, but the baby's breath was a sweet contrast with the poinsettias. Though it wasn't what Elin had wanted, she'd been quick to reassure Delilah that the substitution wasn't going to ruin the wedding for her.

A shadow moved across the floor, and she turned to see what had caused it. Her heart rate sped up when she spotted Tom's bulky form at the door. True to his word, the past four days he'd called her to meet him for coffee and texted her funny quotes at all hours. If this was what courting was all about, she intended to enjoy every minute of it.

Her smile faltered at his somber expression as she waved him inside and hurried to meet him. "I'm glad you're here."

He glanced around. "Looks great. I saw Marc pacing in the backyard. Looked nice in his tux, but he's as white as sea foam. How's Elin holding up?"

"No tears, at least not yet. The dress fits so she's happy. I left Libby in charge of the final details with hair and makeup and came to check on the decorations. Everything looks pretty perfect. I think we're good to go." She consulted her watch. "Guests will be arriving any minute." Her gaze searched his face, and he still hadn't smiled. "Is something wrong? I'm getting an odd vibe from you."

"Someone tried to burn down Vanessa's house."

Delilah grabbed his arm to steady herself. "Is she all right?"

"She got out in time. The doctor is checking her out for some smoke inhalation, but I don't think he's sending her to the hospital. It was clearly arson."

Her knees felt shaky. First the attack on her, and now, one on Vanessa. "You think it's related to the attack on me?"

He put his hand over hers on his arm. "I had to wonder.

Two single women being targeted is a little too coincidental for my taste. I've been going through all the visitor records I can find, but I haven't come up with anything. I've already warned Josh and Alec to be on the lookout today. I'll be at your elbow every minute, but just in case, I want you on your guard too."

"I'll be careful. I checked the guest registry, too, and didn't find a match for the handwriting on the card. What a day for this to happen. I don't want anything to overshadow Elin and Marc's day."

"I'll try not to let it." He reached out and brushed the hair away from her face, then cupped her cheek in his big hand.

The thrill that jolted her was all out of proportion to the simple caress. What was happening to her? All her defenses around him were coming down, brick by brick.

Tom dropped his hand when the back door opened. The first of the guests were arriving with the sunset. Delilah reached over and flipped on the lights. The myriad of tiny bulbs sprang to life in a dizzying array of lights that sparkled around the large space like fireflies. It was so beautiful she caught her breath.

Alec was Marc's best man and he entered with Marc. Some of their Coast Guard friends had offered to usher, so she and Tom moved aside to let them begin to seat the guests. Tom saved her a seat near the front while she went to get Elin.

The night air cooled her skin just a bit as she hurried across the dark yard to the house. Headlights swept the grass as she approached the house, and she recognized Vanessa's car.

When her friend stepped out of the car, Delilah rushed to meet her.

Vanessa had evidently come straight from the clinic. Soot still smudged her face, and Delilah caught a whiff of smoke as she embraced Vanessa. "Are you all right?"

Vanessa clung to her a moment, then released her. "Just shaken. Have I missed the wedding?"

"No, no. I was just getting Elin. If you hurry, you can change and wash your face. You're my size. Take your pick from my closet." She linked arms with Vanessa and turned her toward the house. "The wedding starts in fifteen minutes."

"Yikes, I'll hurry." Vanessa mounted the steps with her.

The door opened as they reached it, and Elin stepped onto the porch in a wash of bright light. Her maid of honor, Sara Kavanagh, was right behind her. Sara was engaged to Josh Holman, and they'd planned to get married earlier in the year. Sara's forced smile made Delilah wonder if Josh was still having cold feet.

"You look gorgeous!" Delilah reached out to straighten Elin's veil.

Elin's hair was in a sophisticated updo, and tiny jewels sparkled in the dark-red strands. Her eyes were as bright as she smiled back at her friends.

Delilah gave a warning squeeze on Vanessa's arm, but she didn't have to worry. Elin was too focused on the wedding to notice as Vanessa went inside and left them on the porch together.

"Marc is going to be bowled over."

Elin smoothed the mermaid skirt over her hips. "You think so?"

"I know so. Let's get you whisked off and ready for your entrance." Delilah steadied Elin with her hand under her forearm as they walked the rough ground to the greenhouse. Sara hurried along behind them. As they neared, the strains from the keyboard playing "Remember When" filtered out the door.

"Is he in there?" Elin's voice was breathy.

"He's right up front waiting." Delilah patted her forearm, then waved over Vanessa who had just exited the house.

Delilah pulled the veil over Elin's face and adjusted it. A string floated at the side, so she pulled out the tiny nail clippers she'd stuck in her pocket for this very reason and snipped it off. "It's showtime. Josie will drop the flowers, then you go, Sara. When Sara reaches the pastor, it will be time for you to enter."

"Don't leave!" Elin grabbed her arm when Delilah reached for the door. "Can you wait with me?"

"Of course." She held open the door for Vanessa to slip inside as the wedding processional music started. Delilah's eyes misted as she watched it all unfold. Was it even possible that marriage was in her future?

SEVEN

THERE WAS NO ONE HERE TOM DIDN'T TRUST, AND HE WAS beginning to relax. He sipped on his punch and balanced a plate of cake and nuts on his knees as he sat in a folding chair and eyed the rest of the guests. The more he thought about it, the more he doubted anyone would try to hurt Delilah in a public setting like this.

Everyone had moved into the large tent for refreshments, and Delilah had strung tons of lights and greenery all around here too. The scent of pine made him eager for Christmas, only two days away. A dance floor occupied one end of the large space, but the music hadn't started playing yet.

Carrying a plate and a glass of punch, Vanessa came across the grass. She had changed into a different blouse, and her face was clean of soot, but her mouth was still pinched and worry lined her forehead.

"Doing okay?" he asked as she settled on the chair next to him.

"Everything is gone, Tom. All my clothes, my computer, my furniture. The fire department got there quickly, but that fire went so fast. I still can't believe it. Who would do that?" Her voice trembled, and she lifted her cup to her lips for a sip of punch.

"I wish I knew. Does Gage know?"

She shook her head. "I called him after I got out, but he didn't pick up. He's in Richmond on business. I'm sure he'll call when he can."

Her boyfriend sold pharmaceuticals and traveled several days a week. It was a heck of a time for him to be gone. He saw Libby's anxious gaze sweep the large space. Her frown eased when she saw her half sister sitting with him. "Libby is worried about you."

"I'm worried about me." She blew out a breath and leaned back.

"Arsonists can sometimes begin as teenagers, so I'm going to talk to the principal at the school and see if there are any troubled guys I should take a look at."

She nodded and picked up her fork, then put it back down again. "I'm going to move in with Libby for now. I'm at a motel in town, but tomorrow one of the guests leaves and there will be room for me."

"I think that's a smart idea." He motioned to Delilah, who was moving around the tent making sure everyone had what they needed.

"Can I get you more to drink?" Delilah peered at his cup.

She looked so pretty in the sky-blue dress that hugged her figure in all the right places. And in the heels, she seemed a different woman than the one he knew.

He pulled his cup away. "No, I'm good. I just wanted to make sure nothing weird's happened tonight. You feel like anyone is watching you, anything making you uncomfortable?"

She shook her head. "And I'm so glad nothing has spoiled Elin and Marc's wedding. It's been a perfect night. I want to keep it that way." Looking over his shoulder, she waved at Pearl, who was corralling all the guests for the first dance. "I think the dancing is about to begin."

Marc's father led Elin to the dance floor, and Delilah smiled as she watched. "They're so lucky to have a loving family."

Vanessa smiled. "Aw, and her mom is dancing with Marc. She's gotten so frail, but she seems pretty bright tonight. Like she knows what's happening."

Elin's mother had Alzheimer's, but so far she'd been able to stay at home with Elin. Marc was so gentle and sweet with Ruby, and she looked up at him with an adoring gaze as he swung her carefully around the floor.

"Did they ever find that lost Cambodian map that Ruby hid?"

Delilah shook her head. "Elin hasn't looked. She thinks it's supposed to stay hidden, at least for now."

Her wistful voice reminded Tom of his search for her brother. He had located a phone number that might be the man he was seeking, but with the fire, he hadn't had a chance to call. Several other couples wandered onto the dance floor as the music changed to an Alan Jackson tune.

Tom put down his refreshments and rose. "I think you need a little whirl around the floor before you get back to work. Just so it's a night you remember for something more than serving cake and punch."

Delilah put her hands behind her back. "I-I don't know how to dance."

"You can't hurt me through these shoes. I'll show you."

A smile lifted her full lips. "Is learning to dance something else your sister forced on you?"

The smooth skin of her arm was warm under his fingers. "You might say that. At the last minute, her best friend's date for the senior prom backed out, and she decided I'd do as a fill-in since I was a star football player."

"You didn't have a date?"

"Nope. Only fear of my sister would have induced me to learn to dance. She worked with me for three days before the prom, and off I went with her friend."

"You sound like you're still close."

They reached the floor, and he led her onto the wood planks. "I don't get to see her often, but we talk all the time. She's married with two kids now. Lives in California with her husband who's a chiropractor." He pulled her into his arms, and she fit just right with her head reaching his shoulder. His hand settled in the narrow curve of her waist, and he rested his chin on the top of her head. "Hmm, you smell good. Sort of like an orange."

"It's the essential oil I use. It's to help me stay calm tonight." Her lips were muffled against his suit jacket.

"Aren't you always calm? You seem to have everything under control at all times."

"It's a facade. I had so little control growing up that I crave it now. But I always fear messing something up." She nestled a little closer. "How about we just dance and I forget that the punch bowl is almost empty and I'm not sure what to do with the leftover cake?"

"I think that's a fine idea." He pulled her closer and brushed his lips over her forehead.

*

The place seemed almost eerily quiet now that the guests had left, and the band had taken their instruments and departed. Delilah had sent cake home with as many people as would take it, and she left the chairs and tent for the rental company to deal with in the morning. The fading taillights of Tom's truck were the last ones to disappear around the curve of the road.

The porch boards creaked under her heels, and yawning, she turned toward the door. It was after midnight, but she felt a deep sense of contentment that Elin and Marc had enjoyed such a marvelous evening. As she reached for the doorknob, she realized she'd left the lights on in the gazebo overlooking the ocean. It would only take a moment to run down and turn off the lights, so she kicked off her heels and went down the porch steps.

She stood on the cold, wet grass a moment to let her eyes adjust to the dark. She didn't mind the chill running up her legs since perspiration dotted her forehead from her exertion in wrapping up the evening. When she could see again, she hurried across the uneven ground. Breathing in the scent of the sea added to her happiness.

The moon glowed in the sky, and the sound of the waves crashing against the shore brought an added sense of contentment. Dancing with Tom tonight had been magical, something she would always remember, even if nothing more between them ever happened.

All alone in the dark night, she realized the gazebo was farther than she had thought. The tiny lights enveloped the gazebo and made it look magical. Alec had built it after he and Libby were married, and the thing was a good twenty feet in diameter. He'd put in screens to help with bugs, and cushions added comfort and color on the wooden benches lining the perimeter.

She went up the steps and whirled around on the floor with her arms out and her eyes closed. It would have been fun to have danced here alone with Tom. She opened her eyes and smiled. No good to her peace of mind was going to come from daydreaming here, so she went to turn off the lights.

The gazebo was plunged into darkness, and she stood for a moment blinking. Gradually, she began to make out the landscape again. The sea foam glowed in the moonlight as it washed onto the beach, and the sound of the sea seemed louder in the dark. Her smile faded. Her deep sense of contentment had been replaced by unease. The hair on her back stood at attention, and she realized she'd been holding her breath.

She let her gaze sweep the area and saw nothing amiss that would account for her sudden alarm, but her breath came fast and her chest rose and fell. She wanted to leap from the gazebo and bolt for the house, but she forced herself to take one lungful of air after another even as she wheeled and headed for the steps.

Nothing here should frighten her, but her hand stole to her pocket, and she wrapped her fingers around her cell phone. Just hearing Tom's voice would calm her down, but she resisted. He'd just turn back around and come to check things out. She'd feel like a fool when he found nothing.

She hurried down the gazebo stairs with her gaze fixed on the comforting bulk of Tidewater Inn rising above the lawn. As she reached the grass, something grabbed her ankle, and she went down with a muffled scream.

Her left arm hit the cold ground, and the air rushed out of her lungs. She gathered her breath for a real scream as panic gathered in her chest, but rough hands rolled her over, and a hard hand smelling of automotive grease clamped over her mouth.

She stared up into a man's face. Something about him seemed vaguely familiar, but she didn't think she'd ever met him.

He hauled her to her feet and pushed her back up the steps to the gazebo. "I told you I'd make you pay. The bill has come due."

She tried to bite his hand, but he had it so tightly against her mouth that she couldn't open her mouth. Struggling against his grip was like a guppy trying to escape a shark. His muscles were massive, and her flailing arms were a puny weapon against his strength.

He dragged her into the gazebo and flung her to the floor, then yanked a strip of duct tape off his arm and slapped it across her mouth. In seconds her hands were bound in tape behind her back. No matter how hard she tried, she couldn't budge the wide strips of duct tape on her wrists.

Fear was a huge beast sitting on her chest. Was this how it would all end? She'd never get a chance to see where the relationship with Tom might lead, never get to smell the sea breeze again, never hear the gulls fighting over fish.

She'd never find her brother now. Tears stung her eyes, and she swallowed the lump in her throat. She didn't want to die.

Scooting away from him, she felt for anything she might use to release the tape, but her head banged against a bench, and she found nothing she could use. Her phone glinted in the moonlight five feet away where it had fallen when he'd tackled her.

He squatted beside her, and with the moon shining on his face, she felt a jolt of recognition. Keith Jacobsen. Though she hadn't met Vanessa's old boyfriend, she'd seen his picture. Clarity came as she stared up into his face. He blamed her for Vanessa breaking up with him.

And he meant to kill her in revenge.

Eight

The pull-off ahead of Tom was a favorite place for vacationers to watch the sunset, but it was also a great spot for watching the moonlit waves breaking on the shoreline. He pulled his truck off the road and dialed the number he had for Delilah's brother, Adam.

The phone rang on the other end twice before a deep voice answered. "This better not be a sales call."

"This is Sheriff Tom Bourne in Hope Beach, North Carolina."

"Sheriff?" The man's voice changed from boredom to interest. "What's this all about?"

"Are you the Adam Carter who lost his parents in an accident when you were twenty?"

There was a long pause on the other end. "That's old news, but yeah."

"You have a sister named Delilah?"

"*Had.* She's been dead a good twenty years."

"She's not dead. Delilah lives here in Hope Beach, and I wanted to find you as a surprise to her."

There was another long pause. "Are you sure this woman is my sister?"

"I'm sure. Like I said, I'm a sheriff. It wasn't easy tracking you down, but your birth dates and parents line up."

Adam's throat clicked on the other end of the line, and when he spoke again, his voice was thick with emotion. "I was told she died in the accident too."

"Who told you that?"

"I didn't even know they died until I got back from a covert mission to Afghanistan. I was told the whole family was in the car when it went into river. I kind of shut down with the news, and it's a little foggy as far as who called. The state police, I think."

No wonder Delilah hadn't been able to find him, and Tom had had such trouble too. If he'd been in Special Ops, he'd probably been wiped off the radar. "She survived in an air bubble in the car. I'd love to surprise her on Christmas Day if you could fly out. Where are you now?"

"I live in California, but I'm vacationing right now in Virginia Beach. I can just drive down there with my wife and kids. I've got two girls." He sounded eager. "I can't believe this! Delilah is alive after all this time. Hold on." There was a muffled exchange with someone, then he came back on the line. "Can we come tomorrow? That's Christmas Eve. I don't want to wait another day to see her."

Tom pictured her face when she saw her brother for the first time and grinned. "That'd be great. She manages Tidewater Inn, a bed-and-breakfast here on the island. I'll talk to the owner and arrange for your lodging. This will mean the world to her."

"You her husband or something?"

"Not yet." Something light and airy spread in Tom's chest. "I care about her though."

"Dude, you're going to be a rock star in her eyes. Mine too. I can't tell you what this means to me, to my wife and daughters. Family. Wow."

Tom's grin widened. "See you tomorrow then." He ended the call and put his phone down. The surprise was going to be so great. His cell phone rang, and as he answered it, he saw Vanessa's name on the screen. "Everything okay?"

"I don't know. I've been trying to call Delilah for half an hour, and she's not answering. Libby turns off her phones at night so I couldn't reach them either."

"Maybe she turned her phone off too." He started the truck and headed it back toward Tidewater Inn.

"She *never* turns it off. A guest might need something. I'm a little worried. It's probably nothing, and like I said earlier, the fire and the attack on Delilah probably aren't related, but after my scare today I'm a little on edge. I thought all my worries were over once Keith left me alone. A lot I know."

Keith. Something clicked in Tom's head. "What was your last communication with him?"

"The usual. That he was going to show me we belonged together no matter what anyone else said."

"Why would he say it that way? Did he know Delilah objected to the way he treated you?"

"Well, yeah. When we broke up, I told him I'd been like a frog that didn't know the water was heating up until my best friend pointed it out." Vanessa's gasp came through the phone loud and clear. "You think *he's* the one who set the fire and tried to hurt Delilah?"

"It makes sense. I'm heading there now. I'll let you know when I find her." He ended the call and tossed his cell phone into the passenger seat.

He'd break the door down to rouse the entire place if he had to. Praying everything was fine, he took the curves at nearly seventy miles an hour, so fast his tires squealed. His heart tried to pound right out of his chest, and he kept pushing away the image of finding her lifeless body. He'd gone through that once with Holly, and he couldn't do it again.

He snatched up his phone and tried Delilah's number, but it rang until her voice mail message came on. So he called his deputy and instructed him to run another check on Keith Jacobsen and to see if Keith's vehicle was parked in front of his house. It would be at least an hour before the deputy could get out there to the house and call him back.

The porch light at Tidewater Inn beckoned ahead, and he accelerated into the final straight length of road, then slammed on his brakes, yanked the truck into Park, and leaped out.

He ran up the inn's steps and rang the doorbell. If he woke up the entire household only to find Delilah sleeping in her bed, he was going to feel like a fool, but he had to know she was all right.

It seemed an eternity before a bleary-eyed Alec, dressed in pajamas and a robe, opened the door. "Tom, what's wrong?"

"Have you seen Delilah? She's not answering her phone, and with everything that's been going on, I was worried."

"It's nearly one in the morning. I'm sure she's in bed." Then he frowned and his eyes widened. "But the door was unlocked just now. And the porch light is on. She usually turns it out when she goes to bed. Let me check. Come on in."

A shudder went down Tom's back and he shook his head. "I'll look around outside while you check." Reversing direction, he went to his truck and grabbed a flashlight, praying all the while that she was safe.

Delilah's arm sockets screamed with pain. Keith had wrenched them behind her back, and no matter how much she tried, she'd been unable to loosen her bonds even a little.

"We would have been happy if you hadn't interfered." His teeth were gritted as he splashed something from a soda bottle around the gazebo. "Even the sheriff can't save you now."

The odor of gasoline burned her throat and eyes, and she swung her head frantically from side to side looking for something to help her get away from this madman. Her nail clippers! They were in the tiny right pocket of her dress, and she didn't know if she could reach them or not, but she pulled her left arm around as far as she could and managed to slide her fingers into the fabric.

The small metallic piece slid away from her, and she sucked in a breath through her nose. The sting of gas in her eyes made them water, but she concentrated and tried to reach just a little farther with her fingers.

Just a little more.

He threw the empty bottle to the gazebo floor where it bounced, then rolled toward her. "Once you're out of the way, Delilah, Vanessa will see how right we are for each other, especially with that idiot Gage out of the way. I've got it all planned out."

Her eyes widened at his mention of Gage. Vanessa had said she tried to call Gage and hadn't been able to reach him.

He must have seen her shock because he smiled. "I cut his brake lines."

The giggle that escaped him raised the hair on the back of her neck, and she struggled to reach the nail clippers again. The nail on her middle finger just barely touched it, and she wiggled on the gazebo floor to push the tiny tool a little higher in her pocket. She managed to pin it between her thumb and index finger.

A tiny flame flared in the darkness. He stared at it with a bemused expression, waving a lighter back and forth. "Fire is cleansing. It will clear out all traces of your prejudice against me and will wipe the slate clean. I can start fresh with Vanessa. Everyone deserves a second chance, don't you think?"

She nodded as she managed to get the clippers open, then

nipped at the duct tape. If only she could talk to Keith. Despair settled in her limbs. She would be too late. He was going to start the fire any second, and the sea breeze would fan the flames quickly.

Her throat burned with the stench of the gasoline as the knowledge of her impending death settled in her chest. Maybe the end would come quickly, and she would wake up in heaven with no memory of what she had to pass through to get there. Maybe there would be enough smoke that she'd asphyxiate before the fire engulfed her.

He turned to stare at her one last time, then knelt and put the flame to the gasoline. A huge whoosh knocked him back on his heels and into a pool of gasoline. In seconds the flames circled his jeans and scampered up his shirt.

Screaming, he rushed through the door and began to roll in the grass. The open door beckoned her as her last possible chance of escape. She tried to stumble to her feet, but her bound feet made it impossible. She'd have to crawl through the flames to escape, and she couldn't do that without setting fire to her clothes.

She worked the nail clippers against the tape again, then flexed her arms. The tape gave a little, and she set the edges of the metal against another area of tape.

Thick, acrid smoke rolled from the flames licking eagerly at the wooden floor, and she gulped in fresh air from a crack between boards in the floor, then saw a bottle of water that had rolled under the bench. If she could get free, maybe she could drench herself in water, then run through the flames.

She worked at the tape again, and the tight bands at her wrist loosened again. Setting her jaw, she put all her strength into releasing her wrists. Her upper arms and shoulders screamed with the effort, but she ignored the pain.

Almost there.

Then her arms were free. She sat up and ripped the tape from her ankles. The smoke was thicker up here with her head three feet above the floor. She choked on the smoke, then reached over and grabbed the water bottle. It was half full. She twisted off the cap, then looked at the fire again.

There was no way she could get through those flames with this little bit of water.

She thought she heard someone shout her name, but it was hard to hear over the roaring of the flames as the floorboards began to burn furiously. Something banged by her head, and she turned to see Tom peering through the screen to her right as the smoke rolled around his head.

"Tom, I'm here!" She staggered to her feet, but the heat was intense, and the smoke was so bad tears instantly filled her eyes and obscured her vision even more.

She staggered toward where she'd seen Tom, but pounding footsteps came from the doorway. A bulky figure leaped through the flames and landed in the center of the gazebo. Tom rolled to a stop, then leaped to his feet and grabbed her arm. Without a word he picked her up, then howling at the top of his lungs, he ran at the screen.

Delilah clung to his neck, and as his shoulder busted through the screen, she kicked at it with her feet. They struck the ground together, but even though Tom's bulk took the brunt of the fall, the air whooshed out of Delilah's lungs. They rolled over and over on the cold grass before coming to a rest. She was atop him with her head cradled on his chest.

Flames licked up the sides of the gazebo, and as they both sat up, she was dimly aware of other figures rushing toward them, of Libby calling her name.

Tom pulled her close and kissed her temple. "Thank God, thank God," he whispered.

NINE

DELILAH'S MUSCLES PROTESTED WITH EVERY MOVE, BUT SHE was too glad to be alive to care. Christmas Eve was her favorite day of the season. The Christmas tree twinkled with white lights, and their reflected glory shimmered off the silver ornaments. Everyone was gathered around the tree and laughing as they exchanged one present each until tomorrow.

Relishing the firmness of Tom's shoulder against her own, she intended to enjoy every moment of a day she didn't think she'd see. He looked impossibly handsome with his button-down red oxford shirt tucked into slim-fitting jeans.

Little Noah had been baby Jesus in the Christmas play at the church, and afterward they'd gathered here at Tidewater Inn. The baby had fallen asleep after getting his Captain Calamari toy, and Alec carried him off to bed, then returned to enjoy eggnog and popcorn with the rest of the group. Libby's Aunt Pearl, Alec's nephew Zach, Vanessa, and her younger half brother, Brent, lounged around the room with their snacks and crumpled paper strewn around the room. Even Gage was here.

He'd discovered the damage to his brake line before he'd had an accident.

Delilah had been shy about giving Tom the book she bought him, but it was now or never. She slid off the sofa and rooted around under the enormous tree until her fingers closed on it. She hid a wince as her burned fingers scraped across the wrapping paper.

A few aches and pains were nothing compared to what Keith was enduring. He was in ICU in Richmond with second and third-degree burns. A guard was outside his door, but it was unlikely he would live long enough to be prosecuted.

Shyness enveloped her as she sat back down on the sofa. "I have something for you." Was she being presumptuous? He hadn't given her a gift. Maybe she was reading more into their budding relationship than he felt.

Or maybe he is waiting on me to show some effort too.

His fingers closed over the package, wrapped in Superman Christmas wrap. "I can't wait to see what you picked." He lifted a brow at the sight of the paper. "Superman?"

"I'd be dead if not for my own personal Superman." She didn't care if he thought she was corny to say something like that. She'd gone to bed thanking God he'd sent a man who cared enough about her to risk a fiery inferno to save her.

Had she chosen a book he'd like? She knew his heart, that he cared about helping others no matter what the cost. Biting her lip, she waited for him to tear the paper off the book and turn it over and reveal the title: *George Washington's Secret Six: The Spy Ring That Saved the American Revolution.*

His grin beamed. "I've been wanting to read this." He dug out his phone and showed her the note with a list of books he wanted to read. The top book was the one in his hand. "How did you know?"

Did she dare to reveal her thoughts? Staring at the emotion in his eyes, she decided if he could risk burns, how could she stay silent? "I know you love history, and I wanted you to read about others who were as brave as you. You're the kind of man who would risk anything for God and country, just like these men. You work quietly in the background to do all you can to hold back the forces of darkness, just like Washington's men."

His face went a little pink. "I wish I had a funny comeback right about now, but I'm speechless." Car lights swept through the window from outside, and he reached over to take her hand. He turned it over and touched the blisters on her fingers. "I think that's the arrival of your Christmas present. It might make you forget about these. At least I hope so."

So that's why he hadn't given her a present yet. "You had it delivered?" She stayed put as he got up to answer the door. Maybe he'd ordered it late. Heavens, he'd been so caught up in keeping her safe, when had he had the time to shop?

"You'll see." He went to the door and stepped outside.

She heard footsteps up the steps and across the porch, more than one set. Craning her neck, she tried to see through the window, but it was too dark to make out much other than it appeared to be a family, probably the late arrivals she'd been warned about. He'd be disappointed it wasn't his delivery. Sighing, she rose to attend to her duties.

Libby rose as well and motioned to her to sit back down. "I've got this. The doctor said you aren't to do anything for at least a week, and I mean to make sure you obey him."

Delilah sank back onto the sofa and took a sip of her eggnog. Two little girls entered the room first. She guessed them to be about two years apart, maybe six and eight. A pretty woman in her late thirties with dark-brown hair entered next, and she smiled as she looked around the room.

Her gaze settled on Delilah and stayed there. "I would have recognized you anywhere. The family resemblance can't be missed."

Delilah smiled back in spite of her confusion. The woman obviously had her mixed up with someone else. She had no family left.

Tom and another man entered right behind the woman. The guy was about forty with dark hair trimmed close to his head in a military cut. He had the erect bearing of a Marine, and something about him caught her attention. He looked like someone she knew, but she couldn't quite place who.

He took a step forward. "Delilah."

His intent gaze disconcerted her, and she rose with her hands clutched together. "Do I know you?" Something about him reminded her of her father, but she couldn't put her finger on it.

Tom shoved his hands in his pockets. "Delilah, this is Adam."

Adam who? Delilah frowned and stared harder at the man.

Then Tom's words took root. *Her* Adam? "A-Adam? You're not my brother."

"You look just like Mom." His voice was hoarse, and he took another step closer. "I thought you were dead, Delilah. They told me you died too."

She took it all in, the curve of his jaw, the cleft in his chin that was like Dad's, the dimple in the left cheek. "Adam." She barely got the word out.

He opened his arms and she went into them. The cologne, Tommy Hilfiger, was the same one he'd worn when he left home. Twenty years had passed, but they all vanished in a moment.

She pressed her face against his shirt and let the tears fall. "Adam, oh Adam."

His hug was fierce, and she could feel the tremble in his arm. A sob escaped him, and she heard him gulp back any more sounds. Lifting her head, she saw him swallow hard, then send an appealing glance toward the woman.

Delilah turned her attention to her new sister-in-law. And nieces. The girls were her nieces. She saw the resemblance now. They looked like miniature versions of Delilah herself when she was that small.

She had family, nieces, a new sister. *And Adam.* She buried her face back in his chest.

"T-This is my wife, Hannah. And our girls, Clara and Eloise."

Delilah lifted her head again but she couldn't speak, couldn't force a single syllable past her tight throat. Tears blurred her vision, and she looked at Tom, who was beaming brighter than any Christmas light.

"You did this?" she managed to choke out.

He shrugged. "Merry Christmas."

She wanted to sweep them all into a hug and hear every single thing that had gone on in her brother's life. Leaving the shelter of his arms, she knelt to talk to her new nieces. Family. What a precious word. Tom had changed her life in so many ways. She glanced back at him and saw his tender gaze filled with so much promise. She was ready to take the next step.

EPILOGUE

Three Years Later

THE COTTAGE TOM HAD BOUGHT DELILAH WAS JUST DOWN the road from Tidewater Inn, so she'd been able to continue her job. From the kitchen window at the inn, she could see the slashes of color from her rose garden while she prepared meals for the guests. With the window open on this late-September day, she could smell the scent of the sea and hear the waves rolling to shore.

She touched the swell of her belly and smiled. She wouldn't be able to work much longer. The baby was due anytime, and Libby only let her cook dinner now. The new girl they'd hired was working out well, and knowing that relieved a lot of Delilah's stress.

Her back ached a bit and she rubbed it.

"You doing okay, honey?" Tom touched her on the shoulder.

She turned and smiled at him. "I didn't hear you come in.

I'm fine, just a little backache. Dinner is in the oven and I'm ready to go home."

Home. Who would have thought she would have a real home with a loving husband and a baby on the way? God was so good. He'd been good before he gave her such an awesome gift as Tom, but every day she was thankful for his gifts.

A sudden cramp hit her in the back, harder this time, and she nearly cried out as her legs gave out under her.

"Delilah?"

Before she could reassure him, Tom had swept her up in his arms and was carrying her out of the kitchen.

"It's nothing, Tom. Just a cramp." But as he reached the parlor, she had to bite her lip to keep from crying out. "I-I might be wrong. I think maybe I'm in labor."

Panic flared in his brown eyes, and he laid her gently on the sofa. Thankfully, the parlor was empty of guests, who were all out enjoying the lovely fall day. "I think you'd better get me home before everyone comes back."

Tom shook his head. "I don't think there's time. Libby!"

Libby's footsteps sounded on the hardwood floors, and she burst into the room. "Is it the baby?"

"I think so. Would you call Amy? Where should I put Delilah? She can't deliver in here."

"A guest suite just down the hall is empty. You won't have to get her upstairs." Libby pulled out her cell phone and continued to direct Tom.

Delilah wanted to tell them first babies always gave plenty of warning, then another sharp cramp hit her and she couldn't bite back a tiny whimper. Come to think of it, her back had been bothering her since this morning.

Tom scooped her up again and rushed down the hall after Libby. Libby unlocked the door to the Tidewater Suite, their most expensive accommodations. Its seafoam-blue walls and calming white linens reached out to embrace her.

She shook her head and tried to protest. "I don't want to mess up anything in here."

"Amy left supplies and instructions. I've got this covered." Libby stripped off the quilt and blankets, then pulled back the sheets. "Hang on." She returned a few moments later with water-proof pads she spread onto the sheets. "Get her into bed, Tom. I've got a delivery nightgown we can get her into if you start getting her undressed."

"I can take care of myself. Tom, put me down." Much to her surprise, he grinned and eased her to her feet. Before another cramp could hit, she yanked off her shirt and sat on the edge of the bed to try to get out of her yoga pants, the most comfortable attire for this late in her pregnancy.

Libby returned with a light-blue cotton nightgown. "Amy is on her way. Fifteen minutes. This is a short one so it will be easy to maneuver during delivery, and you'll be able to nurse in it."

In a jiffy Tom and Libby had her clothed with the night-gown and resting in bed. Just in time, too, because another sharp cramp gripped her back. Tears came to her eyes, and she bit back another groan. She refused to be a screamer.

Tom sat beside her on the bed and rubbed her lower back. "Remember how to breathe, honey."

Of course. This was labor, not some random back pain. She nodded. She was ready for this.

She and Tom hadn't wanted to know what gender their baby was, so this little one would be a complete surprise. Her pulse raced. She would soon hold her baby in her arms. Tom's baby. Our baby.

By the time Amy arrived, the pains had changed and were encasing Delilah's entire midsection. Amy had been a nurse midwife for many years and had delivered little Noah as well as many of the island babies in the past two years. Her brisk, competent manner put Delilah at ease, and she did everything she was told to do.

Two hours later, a tiny red-faced bundle slid into Tom's arms. Tears tracked down his face as he cradled their tiny child in his arms. "Delilah, it's a girl. She's beautiful, just like her mama." He carried her to the head of the bed to place her in Delilah's arms.

A thatch of dark hair topped the red and wrinkled face. The baby screwed up her face and squawked with gusto. Delilah touched her petal-soft skin. "What should we call her, Tom?"

They'd waited to pick out a name until they'd met their little one. Delilah knew the name she wanted, but Tom had waited a long time for this moment, and it was his fortieth birthday.

Tom cradled her tiny head in his big hand and smiled. "Hello, Molly."

"'Star of the sea.' Perfect." And she was. Delilah had so wanted to name her daughter after her mother, and Tom had granted her wish.

So was life, in all its messiness and trials. Life was perfect right now, but Delilah knew there would always be challenges. But challenges brought gifts, too, and the pain was always worth it.

Tom leaned over and his breath mingled with hers as he kissed her. She closed her eyes and soaked in this moment of pure joy.

DISCUSSION QUESTIONS

1. Why do we tend to keep things bottled up about our past? Is there something that's been hard for you to talk about?

2. What does it take for you to tell people about your past hurts?

3. Delilah loved mothering people. Why do you think she did?

4. Have you ever gotten into a rut like Tom and Delilah? What did it take for you to break free and do something different?

5. Have you ever felt the need to prove yourself like Delilah? Why?

THE SUNSET COVE series

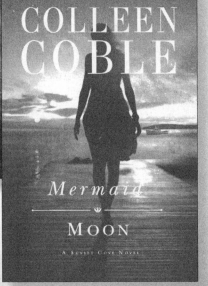

AVAILABLE IN PRINT, E-BOOK, AND AUDIO

AVAILABLE IN PRINT, E-BOOK, AND AUDIO JANUARY 2016

The *USA Today* Bestselling Hope Beach Series

Available in print and e-book

An Excerpt from
The Inn at Ocean's Edge
by Colleen Coble

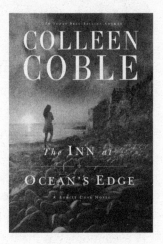

PROLOGUE

July 4, 1989

The sea was near. Though she couldn't see it, she smelled the salt air and heard its roar as it hit the rocks close by. The branches around her held scary shadows. The forest was thick here, and she put her hand on the rough bark of a tree that smelled like Christmas. Mommy had told her to stay far away from the rocks.

But which way are they?

It was too dark to tell. She was afraid to move for fear she'd tumble off a cliff. All she'd wanted to do was go fishing.

She strained to hear her mother's voice, but only noises like screeches and rustling little things in the grass came to her ears. Tears hovered in her eyes and closed her throat. She swiped the back of her hand across her face. Daddy always said crying wouldn't fix anything. It would just make her head hurt.

Mommy would be so upset when she saw her torn dress. Daddy had bought it for her, and he would be angry when he saw her mud-splattered tights and patent leather shoes. Somewhere she'd lost the bow in her hair, and stringy locks hung in her eyes. There was something on the ground, and she stopped and picked it up. A lady's scarf that smelled of flowers. She bunched it in her hand and stepped over an umbrella in her path.

She stopped and cocked her head. Voices? Even though the angry words were just a mumble, she shivered at how mad he sounded. Then she heard a woman's voice, and she moved toward it. The woman would help her. It might even be Mommy.

Tree needles slapped her in the face and made her want to cry even more. But she was a big girl now. Daddy said only babies cried. She pressed her lips together and planted a muddy shoe atop a small shrub to move closer to the voices.

As she peered through the leaves, she saw two figures struggling in the forest. She couldn't see their faces, but the smaller figure fell to the ground, and the man leaped on top of her with his hands at her throat.

"Stop hurting her!" Her eyes widened as soon as the cry left her mouth.

The man turned, and she saw a red pelt tied to his belt. The pointy nose hung at his knees, and she felt dizzy when she saw the red fur. She whirled around and ran as fast as she could, but the steps behind her grew closer. Her climbing tree was just ahead. She grabbed for the limb, and her hand went into the hiding place. She wished it was big enough for her to crawl into herself. She left the scarf in the hole, then reached up for the lowest branch. Her fingers missed and she staggered forward.

Then a hand smacked the middle of her back, and she went tumbling into the pine needles.

ONE

L ike the masthead of a great ship, the stone walls and mullioned windows of Hotel Tourmaline surveyed its island location of wind-tossed waves and rocks. Off the shore and to the southeast of the Schoodic Peninsula, the hotel dominated the island of Folly Shoals atop its pink-granite cliffs.

It had not been easy getting to this remote location. It had taken Claire five and a half hours plus an hour ferry ride from Summer Harbor to reach this rocky shore. She lifted her foot from the accelerator and let her car slow as she took in the imposing hotel, then pulled into the big circle driveway.

A valet, dressed in black slacks and a white shirt, stepped forward to open Claire's car door after she parked her convertible in front of the grand entrance decked out in gleaming brass and glass. She'd kept the top up since the mid-May wind was cool with the temperatures hovering around fifty-five.

Smiling her thanks at the young man, Claire emerged from her white Mercedes and looked up at the five-story structure. Though she'd never been here before, an uneasy shiver went down her spine. She couldn't take her gaze from the parapets with their insets of watermelon tourmaline in the stone around the entry door.

It was like the sea king's castle in *The Little Mermaid*, only on land instead of at the sea bottom. Which was a weird thought to hit her out of the blue. She hadn't seen that old Disney movie since she was a kid.

She recovered her composure and handed the car keys to the valet. "Claire Dellamare, checking in." Reaching over the door of the Mercedes, she grabbed her oiled leather satchel.

"Of course, Ms. Dellamare. Do you have bags?"

The man's voice faded into the distance. Pressure built in her chest as she continued to stare at the hotel. A flagstone walk wound through manicured lawns and disappeared into the shadow of thick forest. She suppressed a shiver at the gloom there. Through the big glass windows, she saw her father standing at the front desk. Seeing him grounded her, and she exhaled.

He would probably not be happy at her unexpected arrival, but she intended to make sure the merger landed them a bigger piece of the aviation pie.

Squaring her shoulders, she forced herself to smile again at the young man awaiting instructions. "There are three bags in the trunk." Without waiting for a response, she hurried past the doorman holding open the entry.

The pink-granite tile floor was unlike anything she'd ever seen. Black veins ran through various shades of pink granite and gave the floor both depth and light. She homed in on her father standing with his back to her and headed his direction, her heels clacking against the stone tiles as she approached the front desk.

The wood surfaces gleamed with polish, and a gilt ceiling arched over the entry area. She'd been in fine hotels all her life, but this one had something special. Just beyond the registration desk, several overstuffed sofas gathered near the floor-to-ceiling windows that looked out onto the forest behind the hotel. She stopped and peered out the window at the trees arching into the sky.

At the sight of the thick pines, Claire thought she might vomit right there on the granite floor. Her breath hitched in her chest, and she tried to ignore the rising panic.

She managed to whisper, "Dad," before her throat totally closed.

It's just the woods. Breathe, breathe.

Her father turned at the sound of her voice. A scowl gathered between his eyes. "Claire, what are you doing here?" His voice bounced off the granite floors.

Her mother had always said he had the voice to charm hummingbirds to his hand, and at the sound of his deep voice, a bit of calmness descended. She forced a smile and brushed her lips across his smooth-shaven cheek, inhaling the scent of his cologne, Giorgio Armani. Her fingers sank into the arm of his expensive suit, and she leaned her face against his chest.

He held her a minute, then released her. "Are you ill, Claire?" He looked at the woman standing to one side of the desk. "Please get my key at once."

"Yes, Mr. Dellamare. I have them ready. Yours and your daughter's." The clerk, an attractive blonde in her thirties, handed over two key card sleeves. "You're in a penthouse suite, next to the one by your parents." She smiled at Claire. "I'm Jenny Bennett, Ms. Dellamare. If there's anything you need, please contact me personally. I'm about to get off work, but my cell number is on my card." She pressed a business card into Claire's hand.

Claire managed a brief nod. "You've been very helpful, Jenny."

The woman had quickly arranged a suite this morning when Claire had made the decision to come here.

"You're staying?" Her father's gaze went to the satchel in her hand.

"I came to help you with the merger." The door behind them swooshed open, bringing the scent of pine to her nose. Her chest tightened again.

"I'm perfectly competent to handle it." Her father took Claire's arm and turned her toward the brass doors of the elevator.

As he led her away from the entryway, her lungs compressed and there was no air. She had to get oxygen. She jerked away from him and yanked her blouse away from her neck. Her purse dropped to the floor, scattering pens, art pencils, lipstick, and a compact across the floor. Her face and neck felt on fire as she bent to pick up her things and stuff them back in her purse.

When she stood, the panic swept over her again. "Can't breathe!"

"Claire, lower your voice." Her father glanced around at the interested guests staring their way.

Her hands and arms tingled, and she couldn't feel her feet. Her father reached toward her, and she batted his hand away. "Don't touch me!" Her scream bounced off the ceiling.

A gray-haired gentleman in a navy suit approached. "Might I offer assistance, miss?"

She backed away, then whirled and rushed toward the entrance. Her feet seemed to be moving in slow motion, and her vision narrowed to a pinpoint centered on the door. Escape. She had to get out of here. Dimly aware of voices calling after her, the door grew closer and closer until she pushed it open and drew in a lungful of salt-laden air.

She leaned her face against the cool stone and prayed for the panic to go away. What was going on? Her left arm hurt.

Her father exited the hotel and hurried to her side. When he started to touch her, Claire flinched. "Don't."

"What is wrong with you? It's not like you to make a scene, to be out of control. This is something your mother would do, not you."

She flinched at the condemnation in his voice. She was *not* like her mother. She inhaled and tried to force her hands not to shake. "My chest is tight and my left arm feels on fire. I'm having trouble breathing. My face is hot. Maybe it's a heart attack."

"You're twenty-nine years old, Claire. It's unlikely it's a heart attack. I think you're having a panic attack. Maybe because this merger is so important. Go for a walk along the beach, and come back inside when you've gotten control of yourself. People will think you're having a nervous breakdown or something."

Though he didn't say it, she heard the implied comparison to her mother again. *Control, I need control.* "You're right. I'll be fine. It was a long drive up from Boston. I just need a walk." The tightness in her chest eased a bit. "Is Ric here yet?"

"Not yet. He's due to arrive tomorrow." His eyes narrowed as he looked her over. "He does like you. Maybe it's a good thing you've shown up."

Her breathing grew easier. "I'm sure of it, Dad. I'll be back in half an hour."

The doorman pulled open the door, and her father disappeared into the bowels of the hotel. The salt-laden air cleared the panic, and she turned to walk down the cliff steps to the waiting sand. The sea would calm her.

Seagulls squawked overhead in a blue sky dotted with puffs of clouds. The wind tugged Luke Rocco's hair and threatened to rip the ball cap from his head as he guided his boat toward Sunset Cove on the south side of the island. He never tired of this view. Though Folly Shoals was just one of about three thousand islands off the coast of Maine, it was a place apart from any other. The grandeur of the sea cliffs, soaring to just under a hundred feet in all their pink-granite glory, always made him feel small and insignificant. Magnificent pines and slender aspen vied for purchase in the rich soil, and wildflowers bloomed in the thin soil.

The engine belched oil and gas fumes that mingled with the scent of the sea, and his boat rose and fell on the waves. His breath plumed out in the chilly air as the sun began its descent over the peninsula. He should have worn jeans instead of shorts today, but the jacket helped. He squinted at his sister. Dressed in white shorts covered with a red sweatshirt, Megan huddled under the Bimini top, which did little to protect her from the cold wind.

He grinned at her. "Smile. At least we got enough fish for supper."

"It's not that." Her thoughtful gaze met his. "I have something to tell you, and I don't know how."

"You're getting married."

She rolled her eyes. "Get real. You've been home three days and haven't seen a boyfriend hanging around, have you?"

Her tone wiped the grin from his face. "You look scared, Meg. You can tell me anything. I won't bite your head off. Does the farm need money? We're about to go broke?" Part of him almost wanted it to happen. Maybe it would wake up the drunken old man back at the house. He'd never been the same since Mom disappeared.

She shook her head. "I think we're turning a profit this year. The cranberry yield looks to be stellar."

"Then what is it?"

The wind tore a strand of hair loose from her ponytail and whipped it into her face. She pushed it out of her eyes. "I got another job offer. It's in Oregon." She rushed on as if she had to spill it all before he interrupted her. "There's a new research facility that's just opened. They're studying viruses and mutations."

His gut tightened, but he managed to smile and nod. "You loved that in college."

Her dark eyes studied him as if to gauge his reaction. "And I'd finally be using that expensive Vassar education."

"It wasn't expensive. You went on scholarship."

She shrugged as she huddled in her red sweatshirt. "You know what I mean. The diploma is worth a lot, and I haven't used it."

"You've used your study of cranberry farming to help the cranberry bogs. That's why we're turning a profit this year." *Shut up, Luke.* She wasn't fishing for a compliment. She wanted to leave Folly Shoals. And how could he blame her for doing what he'd done three years ago? He'd gone to school in Ellsworth and helped with the cranberries, but when she'd come home from Vassar, he'd been only too ready to let her shoulder the full burden while he joined the Coast Guard.

She fell silent a moment, and he took the opportunity to analyze the objections rising to his lips. Pop's recent stroke would prevent him from helping out much. If Megan left, someone would have to pick up the slack. That someone could only be Luke. The thought of dealing with his father soured his mood.

Meg had done it, though. It wasn't fair to expect her to do it forever.

"I see the wheels turning," Megan said. "I know what this means if I leave. I should turn it down."

Her woebegone face made him sit up straighter. "You've buried yourself on this island all your life, Meg. It's your turn to fly. I'm not going to stand in your way. Maybe I can plead hardship to the Coast Guard and get a transfer up here. There's a facility out on Southwest Harbor."

Her brown eyes widened. "But could you do both the bogs and your job? At harvest, it's downright crazy."

"I can try, and maybe we can afford to hire some extra help." He put more confidence into his voice than he felt, but he couldn't let her sacrifice what she really wanted. "If I'd known you weren't happy here, I would have pushed you out of the nest sooner. I thought you loved the bogs and wanted to stay here."

She looked down at her hands, the knuckles reddened from the cold. "I used to. But Pop's gotten even more . . . difficult."

Something in her tone brought him up short. "He hasn't hit you again, has he? I thought he stopped that after I threatened him when I was eighteen."

He'd gotten in their father's face and threatened to call the sheriff if he ever lifted a hand to Meg again. Their dad had taken one look at Luke's face and stepped back. As far as Luke knew, he hadn't dared to raise his hand to her since then.

"It's just been since his stroke. He doesn't mean anything by it. The stroke has left him with a short fuse. He's always sorry after. And he's never even left a bruise."

Luke's fingers curled into his palms. If his dad were here, he wasn't sure he could hold himself back. "I'll talk with him."

Pop had always been difficult, especially when he drank too much. Luke had many memories of nights when he and Megan hid in the closet while Pop raged around the house looking for them.

"There's no need." Meg's eyes held an appeal for understanding. "That's not the real reason I want to go. I can handle a grumpy old man. It's just I'm stagnating here. I'm twenty-eight, and I've never been anywhere except to college. If I stay here any longer, I'll never leave."

He nodded and steered the boat toward the slip. "When would you start?"

"In a month. You'll really help me do this?"

"I want you to be happy. I'll figure it out. That's what big brothers are for."

Her hand swept over the rocky coastline in the direction of their house. "You don't even like cranberries. You were made for the Coast Guard. You thrive on the challenge. And I know perfectly well what's going to happen. You won't reenlist, will you? Even though it's what you've wanted to do your whole life."

"Don't worry about it. I'll do whatever has to be done. I can't let the business just dissolve. It's been in our family for seventy-five years."

She rose on long, tanned legs and leaned against the side of the boat. "And what if he dies? He's been so weak since the stroke. What if you give up your entire life for something that only matters to him?"

His pulse stuttered. "Are you saying you want us to sell the bogs?"

She raked her hand through her short hair, as thick, straight, and black as his. "I want both of us to think long and hard about what's best. Maybe it's time we quit catering to Pop and do what we really want to do."

How had he missed her discontent? And the thought of selling the family cranberry farm didn't settle well with him.

"Let me see what I can do about a transfer, then we'll talk. But no matter what, let them know you're taking the job."

She thrust her hands in the pockets of her sweatshirt. "So now you want to get rid of me and I'm useless, is that it?"

Her voice held no rancor so he just grinned. "Something like that. Your son may love working the land. Or my daughter." Not that he was likely to get married. But the thought of working the bogs unsettled him. He still believed their mom was buried somewhere out there.

Megan reached for the thermos of coffee. "You're thinking about Mom's disappearance, aren't you? Her body's not out there, and believe me, I've looked."

She always could read him. "She has to be somewhere, Meg."

"She's been gone twenty-five years! We'll never find her remains, not up here. It's too remote. Whatever happened to her will remain a mystery."

"Yeah, you're right. But I sure wish we knew what happened." He took a swig of hot coffee. "Ready to head in?"

She nodded.

"Take the helm a minute. I'll get the ropes ready."

She moved to take his place, and he went toward the starboard side. Something floated in the water about eight feet away, and he squinted, trying to make out the markings. "That's a baby orca. Cut the engine."

When Megan complied, he grabbed a paddle and maneuvered closer to the killer whale. The calf lolled listlessly in the water, turning an eye toward him as if asking for help. "It's sick. Skinny too." He scanned the water. "But where's its mother?"

They both studied the horizon and saw nothing. No pod, no mother.

"What if its mother died?" Megan joined him. "We have to help it. We can't just leave it out here to suffer."

"We could put up a sea pen until we can contact an orca rescue organization. I've got some extra netting in the hold."

"But how will you get it to shore? Netting it might kill it."

He shucked off his jacket and shoes. "I'll tow it in."

She grabbed his arm. "Are you kidding? We're five hundred yards from shore, and the water is freezing!"

"I've got this. Just take the boat to our dock. There's already a partial pen along the north and east sides. We'll just have to close the pen on the south."

Megan nodded and went back to the helm. "You sure you'll be okay?"

"Yeah, I'm good." He stepped to the back of the boat and leaped overboard. The cold water took his breath away, and he gasped when his head broke the surface. He waved to show his sister he was fine, then struck off toward the distressed calf. The marine mammal rolled when he touched it, but it was still alive. The skin felt like a warm inner tube, and he caressed it reassuringly. "You're going to be okay, buddy." He hoped it was the truth. This animal was in serious need of attention.

He grasped the orca's dorsal fin and began to tow it toward the sea pen. The calf fluttered its fluke and tried to help, but it was so weak, their progress was slow. His muscles burned, and the cold water quickly fatigued him. By the time he reached the dock, his chest was tight, and he was eager to get out of the water.

Megan had already attached one end of the net and was swimming to meet him. He'd never been so glad to see anyone.

The story continues in Colleen Coble's *The Inn at Ocean's Edge* . . .

About the Author

RITA FINALIST COLLEEN COBLE IS THE author of several bestselling romantic suspense novels, including *Tidewater Inn*, and the Mercy Falls, Lonestar, and Rock Harbor series.

COLLEEN LOVES TO HEAR FROM HER READERS!

Be sure to sign up for Colleen's newsletter for insider information on deals and appearances.

Visit her website at www.colleencoble.com
Twitter: @colleencoble
Facebook: colleencoblebooks

THOMAS NELSON
Since 1798